THE KIRTLAND KILLER

DONALD RUSH

The Kirtland Killer

Copyright @ 2021 by D.C. Rush Books

All Rights Reserved

Without limiting the rights under copyright reserved above, no part of this publication may be reproduced, stored in or introduced into a retrieval system, or transmitted, in any form, or by means (electronic, mechanical, photocopying, recording, or otherwise) without prior written permission of both the copyright owner and the above publisher of this book.

This is a work of fiction. Names, characters, places, brands, media, and incidents either are the product of the author's imagination or are used fictitiously. Cover design by Donika Mishineva. www.artofdonika.com

Table *of* Contents

Chapter 1	Alice Panabaker	4
Chapter 2	Harold Franczyk	26
Chapter 3	The Melonheads	47
Chapter 4	KHS Connection	67
Chapter 5	The Suspect	87
Chapter 6	Gildersleeve	108
Chapter 7	The Kirtland Killer	132
Chapter 8	Another Murder	147
Chapter 9	The First Clue	168
Chapter 10	The Bait	188
	About The Authors	208

Chapter 1

Alice Panabaker

Harold kept staring at the black smudge above him. Not in his wildest dreams would he have expected to see Alice Panabaker at the Great Lakes Mall. He was exiting the main building when he saw her coming out of a blue sedan. Was she back in Kirtland now or did she just come to visit? After all, Harold thought, it's Halloween. Harold concluded that it was the latter. It had been years since he last saw Alice. Heavens must be siding with him, he never thought he'd get a chance with Alice Panabaker. He had initially removed her from his plan. If he was ever going to do this, it had to be now. God knows how many days she was going to stay in Kirtland. The smudge now faded, seemed like a soot stain from a fire burn on the ceiling of his bedroom. It was his mother's room before she suddenly died last year due to a heart attack. What did the witch do to this place? Harold wondered. When she was alive, Harold's mother confined her only child to the first floor of the house. She banned him from coming up. She once said to him that she would kill him if he ever set foot in her room. His mother's death came as a surprise to Harold, but he could not say he was not happy.

Mrs. Anne Franczyk was a nineteen-year-old girl whose dream was to become a lawyer when her parents decided to hand her over to the wealthy Franczyk family— as a wife to their forty-year-old son. Anne's marriage to Jonathan Franczyk meant that she might never be able to fulfill her dreams, and when Harold was born earlier than she'd planned, her reality as a housewife began to unfold before her. Even though Anne never truly settled in as Jonathan's wife, everyone in Kirtland pictured her as the happy wife of Jonathan Franczyk, the millionaire, much so because her parents did a great job of making it look as if it was a love match and nothing like the marriage contract that it was. So, whenever she looked at Harold, she saw a reminder of why she couldn't reach her aspirations. It became worse when Jonathan died. Harold was only six This meant she had to spend more time with him. Before his death, Jonathan was so fond of his son that he would spend most of his time with him— reading books to him, teaching him how to fish or play chess. Anne was never able to hide her contempt towards her son and as Harold became older, he became filled with the understanding that his mother hated him and in turn, he became distant. He kept to himself even more as he grew older.

Now, he is up there in her room and on her bed. What death could make happen, Harold reflected. From his mother's dresser, he picked up the key to the old van that belonged to his father and left the Franczyk mansion.

It is 1968, over eight years since Alice left Kirtland and a lot has changed, she realized. Coming back to Kirtland after all these years meant that Alice was back under her father's sky of expectations. Even though she had made a decent life for herself, and she certainly was not that little teenage girl that left Kirtland without looking back all those years ago, Alice felt like something was still missing. The fog that formed before her in the Gildersleeve Mountains did more to the bundle of uncertainty that hung over her. Alice's father had always tried to mold her into the "perfect" daughter. She sneered lazily as she remembered the day— during her final days in middle school— that she first heard the words "you have to be a role model to every girl in Kirtland" from her father. Words that lingered in Alice's head and later became her father's catchphrase whenever he addressed her. The exact set of words that shaped her teenage life and would later come to fuel Alice's determination to attain perfection throughout high school and beyond. In a quest to impress her father, Alice joined the science club, literary club, music club, drama club, and even the cheerleading team at Kirtland High School during her years, and to be just, she shined at them all. But the pressure to be an exemplar amongst the town girls increased altogether when her father got appointed as a member of the Bishop's Council at the temple during her junior year. With all that she had achieved, Alice knew that she never earned the much-desired respect from her father, especially after missing out on the graduation speech to her best friend, Sunny Griffith. What annoyed Alice now was that after all the years that had gone by, she still wanted her father's approval with the way she lived her life. She wanted her father's endorsement and that was why— if she was to be honest— she decided to come back to Kirtland.

She deliberately chose to visit her parents on Halloween, knowing that her father would be at the Council's conference that was held at the temple every Halloween. Alice steered her way through the forest around the Gildersleeve Mountains and when she reached a familiar spot she smiled, her steel green eyes glittering as memories swept through her.

"Nothing much has really changed, yeah?" she said, looking up at a tree.

At some point during her high school days, Alice picked up smoking but her parents did not notice, not even her mom that seemed to know everything that was going on with her. It was this spot that she would come daily, after school hours, to spend time alone in solitude while smoking away her fears of failing her father. And now she is back in Kirtland, after being gone for almost a decade, and she came to this spot for a smoke even before going home to her parents. Alice pulled out a pack of cigarettes from her denim pocket as she rested her tall, slim body against the hardwood tree. She thought about what she would say, and even more about what her father would say to her after all these years. Instantly realizing she was no longer alone in the woods, she discarded the cigarette, patted down her brown hair, and stepped forward. One of the costumed town kids is trying to pull a scare, she thought. But as the figure coming towards her became more visible, the look on her face said it all. Alice recognized who it was.

***

Harold laid on his mother's bed, tossing continuously until he finally woke up. He heard the sound of crickets so he looked out through the window and saw that it was dawn. The nightmares had not stopped. Nightmares from his high school days that took up most of his nights. That was because his job was yet to be completed, he concluded. He had thought about how he'd felt after his first kill but not once did he think that it would be this gratifying. He felt as if he'd been given a medal of honor.

"Honor," he whispered softly. He was going to get his honor back.

He had previously been worried that with Alice away from Kirtland, he might never be able to achieve that and maybe the nightmares would never stop. But the timing of her return showed that he was on the path to accomplish what he set out to do, and rightly so.

He stepped into the bathroom and picked up a big, brown, leather jacket on the floor. From its pocket he brought out a gold necklace and a pack of cigarettes. Harold didn't know Alice smoked. A lot had changed about her but what didn't change, he realized, was the way she looked at him. Like a dirty pig with no importance attached to it whatsoever, just as she did in high school. Trailing her from the mall, he was surprised to see that Alice wasn't headed home and when he saw her heading into the Gildersleeve Mountains, Harold was astonished. He put the jacket and a pair of leather gloves into the bathtub and began scrubbing. A knot tightened inside him as he scrubbed off blood stains from the gloves, and from there, he knew who his next victim was.

Harold was aware that he needed to be meticulous if he was to pull this off. The body would soon be found and all of Kirtland would be on high alert. But there is no better time to strike than when it was least expected. First, he had to make sure he did not make any mistakes. He had started this and now there was no room for one. Harold went down to the garage and washed the van, then he scoured the floor and washed every piece of clothing he touched since last night.

As the morning light unveiled, Harold became anxious. He was left with a lot of money as the only child of his parents. His father left a lifetime of wealth behind and Harold did not need to work for the rest of his life and was bored. Flashes from last night kept showing up before him and he became restless. He turned on the TV, hoping to catch the first report of a dead body found in the Gildersleeve Mountains but what he saw was the repetition of Brenda Johnson's In Kirtland show. With his eyes fixed on the picture before him, Harold sighed deeply and repeated the name, "Brenda Johnson."

"Kate, wake up!" Dean tried once again, now clear-eyed and seeing that the sun was up. "It's morning already!"

"What?" Kate finally answered.

"Let's go! My mom might start getting worried."

"Relax, it's the day after Halloween. I'm sure even your mom would let you off," Kate said, letting out a knowing smile. "Or are you that eager to get away from me?"

"You know that's not true. Remember, I gotta Show up at the football training too."

Now seated, Kate rolled her eyes. "Okay, let's go. We're gonna have to leave all these behind then," referring to the camp. The previous night, during the Halloween party, Kate had slipped away with her boyfriend just as they'd planned. They came out there in the Gildersleeve Mountains to camp out and spend the rest of the night.

"Hey." Dean held her hand as soon as they came outside the camp and moved closer to her. "I enjoyed every bit of the night with you."

"Me too," she flushed as he kissed her. "At least, let's wash our faces before leaving. You look like you've just seen a Melonhead," Kate said laughing. She knew that he didn't believe in the folklore so she made sure she teased him about it at every chance she got.

Determined to be unyielding, Dean ignored her and started moving towards the stream that flowed all the way to Lake Erie. Kate continued laughing as she followed behind him.

"Kate?!" Dean called out.

"Yeah? Tell me you've finally seen a Melonhead."

"I think she's dead! Oh my God!" he yelled.

"What?"

Shocked by the bizarre sight, Kate covered her mouth as she moved closer. A woman was lying on the ground with her head immersed in the water while the rest of her body was on dry ground.

"We have to tell your dad," Dean said. Kate's father, Randy Horning, was the chief of police at the Kirtland Police Department. "Let's go."

Kate— still in shock— said nothing as they quickly walked away.

While everyone kept busy, Chief Horning stood at a distance, aligning his thoughts. Since he was appointed Police Chief three years ago, Kirtland had been quite peaceful and certainly free of horror cases such as this. It was clear to him that this was a homicide and from his experience of almost two decades. Cases like this spelt the beginning of trouble.

As if to reiterate his thoughts, Officer Mike Bowman— Horning's right-hand man— moved closer to him, "Chief, this has homicide written all over it."

He nodded and asked, "Have we IDed the body?"

"No, we wanted the M.E. to have a first look. He arrived a while ago." Bowman was as confused as everyone at the crime scene. "Everything about this death feels strange, Chief."

"Yeah, it does. But we gotta wrap things up as quickly as possible." He rubbed his face with both of his hands. "Notify Stapleton as soon as the M.E rules it as a homicide, I don't want a case like this hanging over Kirtland for too long."

"Yes, Chief." Bowman sounded like he wanted to say more.

"Mike, what is it?"

He hesitated for a second before he continued, "What if the Melonheads did this?"

The story of the Melonheads was about a legion of mutants from the woods at night with heads the size of melon springs. The stories told about a local doctor who had some tortured patients that he used for experimentation. They later killed him and burned down his house, and since then, they have been in the woods of Kirtland. A version of the stories reported that these mutants attacked drivers who refused to pay a toll on the bridge along Wisner Road while another version said that they feed on babies.

"The what?" Chief Horning sounded, not surprised, but alarmed because the thought had crossed his mind too. But he was the chief of police and he couldn't afford to place homicide cases on groundless stories so he said, "Let's get to work, Mike. The tales of the Melonheads are folktales for kids."

Feeling a little embarrassed, Mike replied quickly, "Yes, sir."

Chief Horning cleared his throat, "Listen everyone, I want to have the whole place scrubbed carefully and anything out of place should be bagged as evidence, even the tiniest piece of metal."

"You heard the Chief, y'all. Let's get to work, lads." Bowman added.

***

The next day, back at the precinct, the medical examiner, Dr. Peralta, established that it was a homicide due to the clear signs of struggles shown by the bruises all over the body. Also, the lines around her neck implied asphyxiation and her hands were tied before she was killed— indicated by the pale lines around her wrists. He reported to the two homicide detectives, partners Jake Smith and Wayne Stapleton. Chief Horning— wanting to get firsthand information— was also present at the M. E.'s lab. The air in the M. E.'s lab reeked of mystification, and for the first time, Stapleton was clueless about a case.

"What was Alice Panabaker doing in the woods?" Chief Horning asked, not exactly directed to any of the other three men. "She left this town years ago when she was a teenager; it's so strange that she suddenly turned up dead in Gildersleeve," he added, now talking to Dr. Peralta.

Dr. Peralta continued his report, pointing to the body before him on a morgue table. "Tests showed that she was smoking not long before she was killed."

"Makes sense," Chief Horning came in. "Forensics found a half-smoked cigarette somewhere not far from the crime scene."

"How far away?" Stapleton asked, talking for the first time.

"Barely a half mile out."

"What about the blue sedan? Has it been established that it belonged to her?"

"Yes," Chief Horning replied. "Her things were all in the car, including her ID. We think she drove the car down there. No other print was found in the car."

"What of footprints from the woods?" Stapleton was half-praying there was one as he asked.

Chief Horning shook his head slowly and replied, "Whoever it was knew better, no footprints, not even the victim's. The killer must have erased them all."

"If that wasn't the original crime scene then the killer carried her all the way down to the stream," Smith started. "Had to be someone strong enough to move the body."

Stapleton held a hand up and said, "Let's not get ahead of ourselves here. What about her parents? Have they heard the news? We should start from there."

Chief Horning shook his head, "No, I wanted to have enough information before paying them a visit." He removed his hat before rubbing his face this time. "I've been friends with the Panabakers for a long time. I'm not sure how to break it to them."

"Also, there is something else," Dr. Peralta went round the table. "Discoloration around the victim's neck suggested she wore a necklace."

"So, are you saying there's a chance that she was wearing one?" asked Smith.

"Yes, that's exactly what I'm trying to say," replied Dr. Peralta. "My guess is gold because high karat gold jewelry has been known to cause discoloration around the skin."

If there was one thing Stapleton had learned throughout his distinguished career, it was never to discard any possibility in a crime case— especially a homicide. So, if the killer went for the victim's necklace, it could be that this was all personal. And in his experience, it was mostly romantic— a cheating partner, an ex, or even an unrequited love.

Stapleton, with folded arms, kept looking at the morgue table and finally said, "If what Dr. Peralta just said is true, then we are looking for someone close to the victim." He adjusted his pose. "It could be anyone, even a lover."

"Most especially a lover." Chief Horning came in. "I have to break the news to her parents, that's if they haven't heard already."

"I'd like to be there while you're doing so," Stapleton was never one to turn down any possibility and this attribute of his was why he was respected among his colleagues— including his partner, Smith. "I'd like to note their reaction to the news."

Chief Horning gave a knowing look but he agreed, understanding Stapleton's move.

At the Panabakers', Chief Horning broke the news to Alice's parents and brother Phil— who was in a wheelchair. In the living room of the Panabakers' house, while the partners studied the family in silence, Chief Horning led the conversation.

"Dan, Phoebe, I want you to know that we are going to do everything in our power to catch the individual responsible for this," the chief said, touching Mr. Panabaker's shoulder.

"She spoke with her mother over the phone last month that she'd visit soon but she never said when. Why would Alice drive to that forest before coming home to us?" Mr. Panabaker was visibly confused. When he woke up that morning, he never would have thought that his only daughter was not only in Kirtland, but laid dead in the Gildersleeve Mountains.

Stapleton spoke for the first time, "To your knowledge, is there anyone close to Alice that you know? A romantic partner or a close friend?"

Phoebe looked at Stapleton, Smith, then she looked at Stapleton again, in quick succession. "I know how this sounds, but we were not exactly close to our daughter."

In between sobs, Mrs. Panabaker told the men about how Alice got into the University of Pittsburgh and had never come home since then. She explained that they were not on speaking terms for a while until she wrote to them one day that she got a nice job in a bank in Pittsburgh and she had decided to settle down there. She told them that Alice did not come home even when they told her about her brother, Phil's accident. After a while, she occasionally phoned and when she told them last month that she wanted to visit, they were all happy that she was finally coming home.

Mrs. Panabaker's sobs climaxed into a heavy wail as she said the last part.

Mr. Panabaker, trying to console his wife and feeling deeply sorry while watching her breakdown in tears, said, "I shouldn't have pushed her so much all those years she was with us. She would still be alive now if I hadn't chased her away with my demanding attitude."

"No, don't say that. You only wanted her to succeed in everything she did, there's nothing wrong with that." It was Mrs. Panabaker's turn to comfort her husband.

Chief Horning sat there next to his friend, anger burning inside him, while he watched Dan and his family as they struggled with the bitterness of the murder of their beloved daughter. Stapleton observed that Phil had not said anything since Chief Horning broke the news of his sister's death.

"Phil, I'm really sorry. I assure y-"

"I don't understand. Why would anyone want Alice dead?" Phil broke in. "I was still a kid when she left Kirtland. Why?"

"Phil, we will do everything we can to find that out," Smith said.

"We are going to need to contact Alice's workplace to find out more," Stapleton proceeded.

"Can you help us with that?"

"Yes, we could do that," Mr. Panabaker replied. "We are ready to do anything you want from us."

Chief Horning stood up and faced Mr. Panabaker, "Dan, I'll let you know about further developments."

The three of them shook hands with Mr. Panabaker and left the Panabakers' house.

Detectives Jake Smith and Wayne Stapleton had been partners for nearly two years. Stapleton was a well-known homicide detective within the police force in Ohio when he was transferred to Kirtland from Cleveland five years ago. In the two years he had been working with Stapleton, Detective Smith had come to understand his partner. He was the kind of man that stretched himself to any extent in order to get to the root of a case. Stapleton was known for having no cold case so far in his career as a homicide detective. Smith had so much respect for him and considered him a mentor.

Just getting off the phone, Stapleton told his partner, "That was Detective Jones from Pittsburgh. He agreed to pay a visit to the bank where Alice worked." He rested, crossed-legged against the table in his office while Smith leaned against the wall opposite him.

"Do you think she might have been followed down there?" Detective Smith asked him.

"I wouldn't rule out anything," he answered. "In fact, after all we know, that seems like the only logical explanation. Except there's someone here in Kirtland who holds an old grudge against Alice Panabaker."

"Or her parents." Smith said, finishing the words for his partner.

"I guess we'd have to pay the Panabakers a visit sooner than we had planned."

A knock drew their attention to the door where a uniformed officer was standing. "A woman is here from the Great Lakes Mall. She claims she saw Alice Panabaker at the mall on Halloween."

"Thank you, Officer, we'll be right there."

The woman was also a member of the Kirtland Temple and she knew the Panabaker's well.

"Mr. and Mrs. Panabaker are very good people. They were so nice to my family when we just joined the temple. I don't understand why anyone would want to do this to them."

Becoming impatient, Smith stated, "Ma'am tell us what you saw exactly."

"Sorry, Officer," she apologized quickly. "So, I went to the mall to get some groceries. And while I was leaving, I saw her in the parking lot leaning against a blue car as she ate ice-cream. It's been a while so I wasn't sure she was the one. But now, with everything that happened, I'm certain she was the one."

"Around what time was that, ma'am?" Stapleton asked.

"Past four, cause my husband came home around five and I got home before him."

"Did you see anyone talking or standing next to her?"

"No, Officer. I don't remember seeing anyone with her."

"Is there anything else you'd like to tell us?"

"No, I'm afraid that's all."

"Okay, thanks for stopping by ma'am." Pointing to the officer that came earlier, Smith said to the woman, "Go with that man. He's gonna give you some papers to fill out. They are just protocol, nothing serious."

As soon as they were alone, Smith said to Stapleton, "Even though she's clueless enough not to know the difference between an officer and a detective, she got the color and type of the car right. I think she did see her."

"Yes, she did."

With this new information, the case just became even more open, Detective Stapleton reasoned. If Alice had gone to the mall first, there was a high chance that the killer followed her all the way through the stops. Or the killer saw Alice at the mall and followed her down to the woods where she got killed. Stapleton told his partner, "We are going to the Great Lakes Mall tomorrow. We're gonna speak with the vendors and ask around if anyone else saw her and after that, we pay the Panabaker's another visit."

Chapter 2

Harold Franczyk

During Harold's days at Kirtland High, there were two sets of students that any stranger in Kirtland would have to be told about before anything else. One of them was, of course, the football team— the Kirtland Hornets. The team had most of the glorious and popular boys and no one messed with them. Boys like Jackson Hayes and Tyron Baker were the stars of the school. The Hornets were on a long winning streak— which made them even more popular and admired. Harold, standing at an inch over six feet with a weight of over two hundred pounds, had thought about joining the football team several times, but he considered himself too slow and uncoordinated. Besides, he thought to himself, the football team is for the popular boys and I'm certainly the exact opposite of popular. Kids called him "fat" and other names and because of this, Harold walked with his head bent down, always avoiding confrontation with anyone. He made sure he was as unnoticeable as possible. But most of the kids knew him because of the family he came from. The Franczyks were well known in Kirtland and their mansion was one of the biggest houses in the town. The second set of students were the cheerleaders, of whom the popular boys picked their girlfriends. Similarly, the cheerleading team was made up of the prettiest girls at Kirtland High School. But particularly, five of the girls were the golden ones. Every student in Kirtland would give anything to be friends with this set of girls. Everyone looked out for these girls in parties and if any party was held without their presence, it was considered lame. The golden girls were made up of Alice Panabaker, Brenda Johnson, Mary Logan, Elise Mckennie and Sunny Griffith— whom Harold had been in love with since elementary school.

Since the first time at Kirtland Elementary School when Harold set his eyes on Sunny, he'd never been able to think about any other girl. Even though he was sure that Sunny did not really know who he was, Harold liked her so much that when he heard that her parents both died in a plane crash in middle school, Harold visited the Griffiths house every day to look at Sunny from afar. He wished he could do more than just stare from afar but he had no other ideas. Harold made sure he knew everything about Sunny. After her parents' death, Sunny's uncle— Paul Griffith— took her into his family and raised her. Harold initially had his reservations about her uncle because his face showed up too often on TV and in the papers and to Harold, people like that could not be trusted. But as they both entered high school, Harold realized that Sunny's uncle— including his family— truly loved and cared for her. They were nothing like his own mother, Harold realized.

Harold's hatred towards his mother deepened as he grew older. He kept to himself even more and he had no friends to talk to. Harold's mother brought home different men and most of them, like this mother, were drunkards. One thing his mother never allowed was their interaction with Harold. She made sure none of the home-less-looking men talked to him. Harold would find himself alone in his room most of the time, drawing images that would be considered inconceivable for a boy his age. Images of different dead people— from a man with his chest gutted to a young girl with a knife through her eyes— filled up his imagination. He made sure no one found these drawings, and since his mom never came to his room, he was never at the risk of being found. The thought of killing his mother and one of her partners crossed his mind several times but he never reached a conclusion as to how to discard their dead bodies without being found. But Harold continued to study everything he could about the human body. He paid attention to homicide news from the papers and local TV.

One day in his sophomore year, Harold came across a magazine cover with the title Instincts boldly written on it. He was drawn to the vivid images of dead characters on the paper and he decided to find out more about the magazine. Later, Harold learned that it was a monthly magazine from a publisher based in New York. It contained different fictional stories including the ones about killers. That was the first time Harold heard about the term "serial killer". The magazine was sold at an expensive price in a local bookstore in Kirtland and only to adults. Getting the money was not the issue, he could easily steal from his mother and she would not even know about it. But no matter how tall and huge he looked, he did not pass for an adult. So, he approached one of his mother's lovers one day, on his way out of their house one Saturday morning.

"A minute of your time, sir?" Harold saw that he was younger than he'd thought, much younger than his mother.

Startled by the sudden approach, the man replied to him, sounding impatient, "Hey, I wouldn't like to get in trouble with your mother. She gave direct instructions not to speak with you."

"Well, you'd be in much bigger trouble if I told her about how you've been stealing money from her."

He was staggered but tried not to show it. He stared at Harold for a minute. "Well, what do you want mate?"

"I want to give you an opportunity to continue stealing from my mother, and of course, buy my silence. All you gotta do is purchase a magazine from the book store."

"And why can't you get this book yourself?"

"Because apparently they would only sell to adults."

"Look here, I'm sure there's a reason why they don't sell the book to kids." The man looked really troubled.

"Sir, I'm sure my mother will be interested about how you got that money peeping out your pocket," Harold shot at him.

He looked down at his trousers and quickly adjusted, pushing back the drifting note.

"Okay," he finally agreed. "What do I gotta do?"

"Meet me here by 4pm today. Do not be late, sir." Harold handed him a note.

Since then, it was not hard to convince him to get subsequent issues of the magazines until Harold's mother stopped seeing him. But Harold continued to pay close attention to anything that involved killing. He would stay up all night and think about scenes of him performing all that he had learned. Sometimes he put them down in drawings, but most times, he just let his imagination flow. By the time that Harold got to his senior year at Kirtland High, he had developed a moderate understanding of how he could take a life but his knowledge was yet to be put to practice.

Harold was seen by other students as a weird kid who never talked to anyone in school. He had no friends and he never talked in class. Although Harold was highly intelligent and smarter than most of his peers, his grades were average. Sometimes a teacher would ask a question that Harold knew the answer to but he never answered. Harold was shy and he did not know how to communicate with other students, even though most times, he wished that he knew how. He never really cared much about school but he did not miss a day of school because of Sunny.

While Harold continued to follow Sunny's life from a distance, she grew to become the most admired and popular girl in Kirtland. She was the girl that every other girl wanted to be like, even the teachers liked Sunny. Sunny and Alice were the closest of the five friends. They seemed to be around each other at all times. If there was one thing Harold could change in Sunny's life, it was to stop her friendship with Alice Panabaker. To Harold, girls like Alice meant trouble. They thought they were smarter than everyone else and they saw boys like him as suckers who had nothing to do with their lives. Alice would go on arguing with teachers during classes and she always made sure she won every argument she found herself in.

One day during a chemistry lab period at Kirtland High, the teacher, Mr. Wright, organized a competition among his students— which included Harold and Alice. He instructed them to form groups and he assigned to each group an experiment to perform. Mr. Wright told them that any group that succeeded by finishing first won the competition. Harold saw that no one wanted to be in the same group with him except a couple of kids that were not in the least interested in chemistry and could not care less about which group they ended up in. He was then determined to win the competition and show them that he was not the dumb, weird kid that they thought he was.

Twenty minutes into the experiment, Harold said to the two unconcerned kids in his group, "All we have to do now is wait for a couple of minutes while the solution heats."

Unexpectedly, Alice sharply walked past them, leaving Harold to find most of their apparatuses displaced, including the beaker— now shattered— that contained the chemical solution.

Still shocked by the turn of events, Harold looked up to see everyone staring at him as he stood before the mess.

"Mr. Franczyk, I'm sure you are aware of the laboratory code of conduct," Mr. Wright said. "We don't tolerate any careless use of lab equipment."

"You don't win by messing up the whole thing, Harold!" Alice yelled out loudly.

The whole class laughed at Harold, even the two kids with him could not help their giggles.

An embarrassed Harold immediately ran out of the lab. He had never felt so humiliated in his life.

When he got home that day, he cried so much that his mother noticed and asked him what was wrong. He said nothing of all that happened earlier in school and only replied with, "I just want to be left alone."

"Well, suit yourself then." His mother got into her usual self and left him alone.

Since that day Alice Panabaker continued to torment Harold. She called him different names— weirdo, monsterbag, douchebag— whenever he walked past. Gradually, Harold built up a load of contempt towards Alice. He came up with several drawings of a dead Alice, portraying her fictitious death in different versions. What made it harder for Harold was the fact that Alice and Sunny were always together, even when the rest of the girls were not with them. He wished he could show Sunny what type of selfish and arrogant person Alice really was.

***

Sunny was really shaken up when she heard the news about Alice's death. She was shocked to find out that Alice was back in Kirtland through her death. When Alice left Kirtland, she left everything behind, including her best friend. Sunny tried reaching out to her a couple of times after that but it was apparent that Alice did not want to have anything to do with Kirtland. She did not understand why Alice shut out on her like that. Now, she might never get the answers to everything she wanted to ask her. Since she saw the news on TV, Sunny made sure she was always around people. Sunny's uncle was the mayor of Kirtland and Sunny worked as his assistant. She had buried herself in work because she did not want to sit down and think about why someone would want to kill Alice, and mostly because it scared her to imagine that someone that used to be so close to her was found dead.

Now, as she stared at the old wall clock that hung at the Panabakers' living room with its two dangling rings moving rhythmically as the late fall wind blew into the house, she thought about the time she spent with Alice. All their days at Kirtland High where they did everything together, the sleepovers, the days they spoke to each other about their dreams and the times they spent together talking about boys. Tears rolled down Sunny's left cheek, she could not still believe that Alice was really dead.

Phoebe Panabaker came out with a glass cup and a bottle of wine. "Sorry for taking so long, Sunny." She placed the items on the table. "I had to go fetch the wine from Dan's little cellar." She tried to smile. Sunny, wiping the tears off her face replied, "It's okay Mrs. Panabaker. You really didn't have to do this."

Phoebe moved closer to Sunny and held her hand. "I know how close you two were before she left. How hard it must be for you." She hugged Sunny tightly.

Sunny saw how much she must be missing her daughter. Holding her like that made Phoebe feel a little closer to her child once again. Sunny could not control the tears.

When she finally sat back, Phoebe asked her, "I'm sure even when she wasn't talking to any of us, she got in touch with you. Did she tell you she was coming to Kirtland?"

"No, she didn't."

"But you guys talked, yeah?"

"Yeah," Sunny lied. "Once in a while."

She knew she was not supposed to but with what just happened, she wanted to make her feel better. Even if it meant lying to her. When her own parents died years ago, she was still a young girl. But as she grew older, she realized how much she missed them. Even though her uncle and his family had been there for her, Sunny still felt like a big part of her life was missing. So, she understood how Phoebe Panabaker felt and she wished she could make it all go away.

The knock on the door was a welcome distraction for Sunny. She was getting emotional and might have broken down in tears if it had not come.

Detectives Jake Smith and Wayne Stapleton were allowed in by Phoebe. Smith strolled in first, wearing a sky-blue shirt on a navy blue trouser with suspenders. Figures in the police considered him a fitting partner to Stapleton. Most of their colleagues called him the younger, livelier version of Stapleton. Smith liked the fact that he was likened to someone as revered as Stapleton but he knew they were two different people. Stapleton was deeper in character, more insightful, and of course, more experienced. Stapleton was in a brown khaki and a white shirt. He was the first to speak.

"Hello, Mrs. Panabaker," he said. "Sorry to come in without prior announcement. We just have a few questions we'd like you to answer."

"Of course," Phoebe replied. "But Dan is not around. He took Phil to the clinic. He had an appointment."

Stapleton looked at Sunny, waiting for Phoebe Panabaker to introduce the younger woman— whom Stapleton perceived to be around the same age as Alice. Phoebe, getting the cue, got on with the introduction. "Detectives, this is Sunny Griffith, she used to be Alice's best friend before she left Kirtland." Then to Sunny, "These are the homicide detectives in charge of the case."

"I don't know if you're aware Mrs. Panabaker," said Stapleton, "The person responsible for this was specific about the way we found Alice's body. Can you think of anyone you've had a quarrel with recently?"

"Detective," she said, "Dan and I are easy-going people. It brings me sorrow to think that someone wanted our daughter dead. We just wanted... "

Phoebe broke down in tears. She could not believe what was happening to her life. Sunny moved closer to her and patted her back. Tears took form in Sunny's eyes; she could not bear it either.

"If my memory serves me right, you are the mayor's niece and assistant, yeah?" Smith asked Sunny.

"Yes, he's my uncle and I work for him," she replied.

"Well, since you are here, you might be able to help us out with some answers too," Stapleton said. "Just some background information. Since you were close to Alice before she left Kirtland, anything you know could potentially be of help."

"Yes. Sunny probably knows more than we do," Phoebe cut in. "Alice kept in touch with her all this time."

"Not like that," Sunny said. "Just once in a while and Alice didn't like talking about herself. We only chatted about random stuff."

Stapleton noted Sunny's hesitation and tried to dismiss it as nervousness due to the circumstances surrounding the death of Alice. But he knew that nothing could be ruled out. So, he asked, "Ms. Griffith, were you aware that Alice was coming to Kirtland?"

"No. She didn't mention anything about that." Sunny replied.

"That's odd. A month earlier, Alice told her mom over a phone call that she was coming. I would have thought that she'd tell you about it, too." Smith said, having a similar feeling to Stapleton's.

"Maybe she didn't want to tell Sunny since she wasn't sure when she was coming," Phoebe Panabaker said quickly, forcing a smile. She did not like the feeling she was getting from the men. Sunny was the last person that would want Alice dead and no matter what fight they had going on, she believed that Sunny would come to her first, like she did when they were in high school. "Gentlemen, the news of Alice's death is as grievous to Sunny as it was to us. The girls were inseparable before Alice left."

"No, I completely understand. They are just trying to do their job," Sunny said.

"Thank you, ma'am," Smith replied.

Outside the Panabakers' house when the detectives were leaving after they had tried to find out from Phoebe if there was anyone that she could think of that might harbor ill-feelings towards them, Sunny ran up to them as they were about to enter their car.

"I'm sorry about this but you have to know that Alice and I never got in touch," she said. "I tried writing to her after she left, but I never got a reply." She looked down, feeling embarrassed for lying. "Moments before you came, Mrs. Panabaker assumed I was in contact with Alice and it comforted her to have someone close to her daughter there with her," she continued. "I didn't want to ruin that for her. I hope you understand." Sunny saw the look in Smith's eyes, so she added, "My parents died in a plane crash, and even though I was still a kid, I understand how it feels to lose a loved one."

"It doesn't change the fact that... ," Smith started but stopped when Stapleton raised his hand.

"Thanks for coming to us," Stapleton said. "I understand your intentions but it's important that we know the truth about everything if we are to get the person responsible for this."

"I agree and I'm sorry," Sunny replied. "Thank you."

"We'll keep in touch."

The men got into the Kirtland Police Department's Chrysler Newport and drove away.

***

Detective Jamie Jones refused to sit down when the woman at the city bank in Pittsburgh offered. His black leather jacket— with his initials "J.J" inscribed on the left chest— dazzled in snow-white lights that lit the city bank's lobby. Many thought that rather than pursuing a career in the police force, he should have considered modeling for fancy fashion brands. However, if there was one thing that Jones was more invested in than fashion, it was his work. He stood there, thinking about the case, at least from what Stapleton told him over the phone.

Why would someone suddenly end up dead in a town they had left years ago? Could someone have been patient enough to wait for her return or did someone follow her all the way from Pittsburgh? This is definitely a puzzling one, Jones thought.

A short, warm-looking man wearing a grey suit approached him. "Good morning. You must be Detective Jones from the Pittsburgh Police Department," he said, extending his hand.

"Right." Jones replied.

"Luke Bells, head of HR," he said. "Please come with me."

Jones followed him into an office that looked rather scanty except for an open shelf that contained piles of documents and some other furniture.

He offered Jones a seat. This time he accepted.

"We were shocked to hear the devastating news about Ms. Alice. She was one of our brightest accountants. Please tell us what we can do to help."

"As you know, the victim died in Kirtland and I'm here on behalf of my colleagues in Kirtland," Jones said. "I'd like to get her residential details and other information. It would also be nice if I can speak with the people that worked closely with the victim."

"We can make that happen," he replied. "We all loved Alice, she was success-driven. In fact, she had been a key figure in this organization in recent years. It's hard to think of a reason why someone would want her dead."

"Why did she say she was leaving before she left?" Jones asked.

"Last week, she asked for permission to take a week away. Actually, Alice's team recently wrapped up a big deal of which Alice was a key player in making that happen. It made sense because she worked really hard for that deal and we thought she might need some time off."

"The members of her team, let's start from there." Jones said.

Stapleton stared at the board before him. Everything they knew so far was highlighted on that board but something was missing. He knew that but he could not quite figure it out, yet. Smith shared his partner's perplexity. The information before them— including what Jones found out— was insufficient to make a conclusion. From what they had learned, Alice Panabaker had no friends outside work and no romantic partner that anyone knew of. Even her neighbors confirmed the nonexistence of Alice's social life. All she did was bury herself in her work and at twenty-six, Alice apparently had a lot of money for her age.

Smith turned to his partner. "Someone is doing a good job of hiding something from us," he said. "I think we should visit Pittsburgh and find out who."

Stapleton had thought so much about it too, and that would, as a matter of fact, make a lot of sense. But what he feared was that the culprit resided there in Kirtland. If that was the case, he reasoned, then the killer that they were looking for was a very dangerous personality who had the patience to nurse an intent for almost a decade. And most especially, why did the killer stage her body that way? Was a message being passed? Stapleton picked up photos of the scene and studied it once again.

"How's the profile coming up, Jake?" Stapleton asked.

"Nothing new has been added. Male, at least six feet, substantial physical strength suggests a more than average build," Smith replied.

Stapleton nodded and continued, "Alice left Kirtland months after her graduation from high school. I think it's time we dug into her life before she left."

"Who was Alice Panabaker eight years ago?" Smith repeated after his partner.

"We are going to find that out and I won't cease until I get my hands on this psychopath." Stapleton answered.

Chapter 3

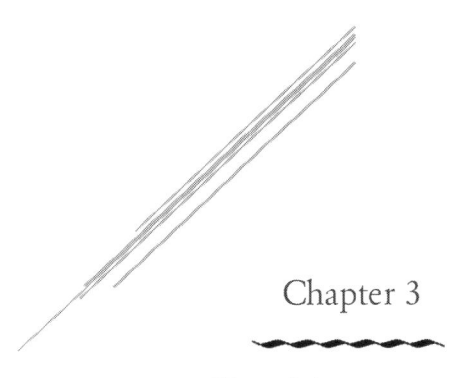

The Melonheads

It's been four days since Alice's body was found in the woods of Gildersleeve. Harold sat down on the brown sofa in the Franczyk's living room, watching the inhabitants of Kirtland on TV as they voiced their contrasting opinions about the Melonheads. The mysterious murder of an old resident of Kirtland— who had not stepped foot in the town for a very long time— made many to conclude that the tales of the Melonheads were true after all.

A man who identified himself as a farmer said, "This is dearly the work of the Melonheads. We've all heard the tales about these mutants and now it is evident that they are true. They weren't made up; it is here before us and something has to be done."

Another woman— a nurse— disagreed and said, "Someone killed that young woman and we'd be letting them get away with it if we put it on the Melonheads."

There was a time when Harold believed in the stories himself. When he was younger, he drew several images of Melonheads, with their enlarged heads and mutated faces just as he heard from the stories. But as he grew older, he became indifferent to the tales. In fact, so many things had changed for Harold. He was no more the kid that— according to Brenda Johnson— had more than his fair share of flesh and certainly not the boy that walked around uncoordinatedly with his head bent down.

After he left Kirtland High, he was determined to shake off the shame and degradation that accompanied him all through his younger years. Over the years, Harold worked hard physically to get himself in the shape that he was. Anyone that saw him would not have believed that he was the same Harold Franczyk. For this reason, Harold was almost distracted with astonishment when Alice Panabaker recognized him in the fogs of the Gildersleeve Mountains. Just for a split second in the woods, a strain of anguish wiped through him when he realized that a part of the boy he had worked so hard to leave behind still identified with him. If he was truly going to complete this transformation, Harold told himself, he had to get rid of them all. It was the last phase of his evolution and he had to do it. But one thing that lingered in his life was loneliness. He had always been lonely and even more so since his mother passed away. Harold feared that he might never be able to overcome this. Distressed by these thoughts, he turned off the TV and left for his room. In his room, he grabbed his drawing materials and started sketching what looked like dry land beside a water body.

***

Having grown up as the only daughter in her family with three brothers, Brenda Johnson had learned everything about standing up against any group of men in order to get what she wanted. In just over four years of working at the local TV station in Kirtland, she worked her way up the ranks and became the anchor of In Kirtland — a show that aired twice every week, highlighting different happenings in Kirtland. Sometimes, when an incident such as a murder case occurred, the show detailed the facts around that incident and brought it to the viewers. Now, a murder case was garnering the attention of everyone in Kirtland and they wanted to remove her from the show that she had helped popularize. She was not going to take any of it. The director of the TV station, Mr. Groff had called her earlier that day into his office to tell her about the "new development".

"Come on in Brenda and have a seat," he said, as Brenda opened the door to the old office that seemed to permanently have the smell of food hung all over it. "Yeah," he continued. "I want to inform you about a new development concerning the In Kirtland show." "What new development?" Brenda asked. "Well, because of the new happenings in Kirtland, especially the murder case," Mr. Groff said, clapping his hands as he completed his phrases. "We have decided to remove you from the show on a temporary basis so that our more experienced presenters could come in and handle the intensity that the events require."

Brenda could not believe her ears. She certainly was not going to allow them to take the show away from her. Not when it mattered the most. But she calmed herself and asked him, "Who's gonna be anchoring the show?"

"Dom and Franklin," he replied. "We have decided to double it up. This is just a temporary set up. I hope you understand. The show will be back in your hands after everything has died down." Mr. Groff added, smiling at the completion of his speech.

Brenda understood what the management team was trying to do. Prior to her taking over the show, it was scheduled to be canceled because it was not getting enough views. But they decided to give her— a rookie presenter— a chance to revive the show after she presented the management team with her impressive ideas about how she could get the show to start doing well. Now that she had made it the most watched show in Kirtland, they wanted to steal it from her.

She stood up and replied to Mr. Groff, "I worked so hard to bring the show up to this level and I'm definitely not gonna allow it to be taken from me, especially now. So, Mr. Groff," she added. "You can tell your glorious boys not to bother. I will continue to be on that show."

It was past ten but Brenda did not feel like sleeping, she kept thinking about the conversation with Mr. Groff. How could they do that? she kept asking herself. She wandered into the kitchen to make herself a cup of coffee. While she was drinking coffee, she thought about Alice's death. She did not know what to think. How could Alice have suddenly ended up dead in a forest? Maybe the Melonheads really killed her, she concluded. She remained in the kitchen for a while after she finished her drink. It was her favorite part of the house, a two-flat bungalow owned by an aged woman left behind by her deceased husband. Brenda used to love cooking but she did not get to cook as much since she started working at the TV station. She had worked so hard and sacrificed so much for this, she reflected, again, as she put off the light and began heading towards her room.

Suddenly, a huge figure appeared before Brenda, grabbed her and muffled her scream with his large hands. The leather glove tightened as she tried to wriggle herself free. The stranger dragged her into the room where she found it hard to keep her eyes open just after a sharp-smelling substance was brought close to her nose.

Brenda's eyes opened from what seemed like a short dream. It was the sharp smell again, she realized. She felt really cold and her limbs felt dead. Where am I? she asked herself. It took her a moment— and the figure appearing before her again— to remember. She recalled that a huge figure came into her house and attacked her. She realized that she was tied up. No wonder her limbs felt that way. Was she being kidnapped because of the show? She could not believe they would go this far. She mumbled something but the figure had taped off her mouth.

"Hello, Brenda," the voice sounded too soft to belong to the huge figure before her, almost like a child's. "Remember me?"

Harold pointed a small torchlight to his face and moved closer to Brenda. He wanted her to know that he was the one that was going to kill her. Finally recognizing the huge figure as Harold Franczyk, she became more confused than scared. She had supposed that Mr. Groff and his boys had hired a kidnapper to threaten her. She had not seen Harold Franczyk for a while. The last time she saw him was when she went on-site to report a car accident that happened near the Franczyk mansion.

Harold studied Brenda as she twisted swiftly in protestation. He had thought about this several times. Harold had planned to kill her first, before he changed his plan when he unexpectedly saw Alice Panabaker at the mall. Brenda Johnson was the quintessence of why he began his mission. She made Harold's life miserable in high school and now she was going to pay for it with her life. Harold brought out a security chain from his leather jacket.

"This is for all those years you made my life miserable in high school, you slut!"

Brenda sunk into fear. She was going to die, not because of Mr. Groff or his boys, but by the hands of Harold Franczyk. Even in the dark, she could see the menacing look on his face. He really was going to kill her.

Harold brought out the chain and wrapped it around her neck. He tightened the chain, groaning as he did, until there was no life left in Brenda Johnson to fight anymore. He had expected her to be exactly that way— the Brenda Johnson who was always ready to fight. The gratification that flowed through Harold was what he had been craving for all those years. The powerless and vulnerable look on Brenda's face when he brought out the chain was going to stay with him forever.

***

Harold's senior year at Kirtland High left him with the deepest scar. At that point, he had already concluded that he and Sunny were meant for each other. He believed he knew enough about her now and he was fed up with watching her from afar. He slowly built up his confidence and decided one night— after he had just heard his mother come into the house with one of her young lovers— that he would ask Sunny out on a date. The large collection of Sunny Griffith's drawings that he had were not enough anymore, he saw that he needed to make a move. He was aware that Sunny was dating Jackson Hayes of the Kirtland Hornets. Jackson Hayes was the most arrogant person Harold knew. He acted as if he owned the school and to Harold, he was also the dumbest boy at Kirtland High. He did not deserve Sunny. It saddened Harold to see them together and anytime he did, he wished he could make Jackson Hayes disappear forever. Jackson was the quarterback and captain of the Kirtland Hornets which made him the most popular boy at Kirtland High. Harold believed that Sunny did not really love Jackson but he was the captain of the football team while she led the cheerleading team and that probably made her agree to dating him. Harold was determined to make her realize that she did not need Jackson Hayes but first, he needed to ask her out on a date.

After observing Sunny for a whole week, Harold never got a chance with her alone. When she was not in class or with her friends, she was with Jackson or at practice. It was on a Monday afternoon, after school, when Harold decided to walk up to Sunny. She was standing before her locker, chatting with Brenda Johnson. Harold had known Brenda Johnson since childhood. Their house was not that far away from the Franczyk house. When they were younger, he often went to their house to play with her brothers. Alice's bright smile warmed Harold's chest as he looked at her and he thought about how nice it would be to run his hands through her long blonde hair.

He went forward to them. "Hi," he said as the girls turned to him. "I'm Harold Franczyk." He lifted a hand to hide his nervousness. They looked at each other in amusement and it made Harold even more uneasy.

"Hello," Sunny replied. "I know who you are."

Harold could not hide the delight in his face. All the times he had simulated the occasion in his head, never did he, for once, consider that she might know he was.

"Would you like to go out on a date with me?" he asked.

Brenda burst into a loud laughter that made everyone around turn their attention to them.

"It's really nice that you asked me out, Harold. But I have a boyfriend so I can't go out with you. I'm really sorry," Sunny told him.

Everyone was looking at them and Harold wished that he could vanish into thin air. He found it hard to control his breath and something seemed to knot his lungs together. His head was ringing inside and he felt like it would burst open.

Brenda Johnson continued her laughter, then she said to Harold, "Why would you think that she'd go out with a scumbag like you who has more than his own fair share of flesh?" Another round of laughter erupted out of Brenda and everyone joined her this time. Sunny did not say anything, she just stared at Harold. "Guess who's trying to ask a girl out?" Brenda said again. "It's Mo-Mo!"

"What the hell is a Mo-Mo?" asked one of the students.

"It stands for Missouri Monster! Scotland has the Loch Ness Monster, Washington has their Bigfoot and Kirtland has the Missouri Monster!"

The other kids laughed again, with many of them repeating the new nickname that Brenda Johnson gave to him. Harold stared so hard at the floor, he wished it could open and sink everyone around. He ran out of the office and cried all the way home.

When he got home that day his mother was just leaving the house with her man as he was about to enter. When she saw his face, she asked him "What's happened? Were you crying?"

"It's none of your business. Leave me alone!" Harold yelled at her.

The man stepped forward. Harold saw that he was older than the others. Maybe mom finally decided to stay with someone around her age, he thought.

"That's no way to talk to your mother," the man said.

"That's definitely none of your business either. Get out of my house, you thief!"

"Harold!" his mother called before the man landed a slap on his face.

The pain was sharp and fast. Harold looked at his mother and when he saw the first sign that she was not going to do anything, he held up a fist and placed a blow on the man's jaw. The man fell off his feet immediately and Harold realized that he was drunk. Then he left for his room.

In his room, Harold pulled out all the drawings of Sunny Griffith that he had and tore them apart. He was mad at Sunny for rejecting him because of Jackson Hayes. He was mad that she did not say anything while Brenda Johnson humiliated him before the whole school. He was mad at his mother for bringing him into a lonely world where everyone, including her, hated him. But ultimately, he was mad at himself for thinking he could ever get a chance with Sunny Griffith. He was humiliated by his own stupidity and that moment marked the beginning of his evolution. Harold skipped school the next day and when he finally went back to school, he was confronted by Jackson Hayes.

The whole school— including Jackson— had heard about the incident. Jackson along with several other members of the football team walked up to him. "Hey Franczyk, where have you been hiding out? Heard you are trying to steal my girlfriend," Jackson said. "You must really have some guts to do that. Show me what you've got, Mo-Mo." He pushed Harold.

Tyron Baker and the other boys laughed and echoed after him, "Show us what you've got, fat kid."

"I don't want any trouble. You guys should just let me be," Harold said. Harold was taller than any of them and if he were to fight any one of them, including Jackson, he knew he would come out on top.

"You heard the man y'all, he doesn't want any trouble. Let's go guys." Jackson acted like he really was going to leave him alone but turned around and punched him. The others held Harold while Jackson Hayes beat him up. Harold wriggled free and lunged at him, he broke Jackson's nose with a hard blow to his face.

"Stop!" Harold heard Sunny's voice as he was atop Jackson Hayes, hitting him. He stood straight and stepped back as Sunny rushed to him. Jackson's nose was covered in blood.

"What did you do to him?" She faced Harold.

Anger burned through Harold but he could not utter a word, so he left.

Later that day, Harold was summoned into the principal's office where he met Jackson Hayes and Tyron Baker, already seated before the principal, Mr. Dickson.

"Mr. Franczyk, it was reported to me that you were involved in a fight against these boys. This is very unusual for you, tell me what happened," Mr. Dickson said.

Harold, raging with resentment for the two boys, looked at them before he yelled, "They attacked me first!"

"Liar!" Tyron Baker yelled. "He broke Jackson's nose."

The door opened behind Harold. Brenda Johnson and Mary Logan came in. Harold knew Brenda was Tyron Baker's girlfriend. And he once saw Mary Logan and Jackson kissing at the school's car parking lot after school.

"We were both present at the scene, sir," Brenda said, "Harold punched Jackson first because Jackson's girlfriend, Sunny, refused to go out on a date with him. He also beat up Tyron while he was trying to separate them."

Harold was left with disbelief at the lies that the girls made up. He was breathing so loudly that the girls stepped back from him, scared that he might attack them.

Eventually, the girls' lies were sufficient to instigate a punishment for Harold. He was suspended from the school for a week while Jackson Hayes and Tyron Baker got off with a two-day detention.

Three days into the week-long suspension, Harold's mother finally noticed that he had not been going to school. Harold was just walking out of the kitchen when she saw him.

"Why are you not in school, Harold?" she asked.

"I got suspended," Harold replied indifferently.

"Suspended? Why?"

Harold ignored her and went into his room. He expected her to let it go. After all, she never really cared about anything that has to do with him anyway. Besides, Harold liked being away from school, especially now that Brenda Johnson had made a mockery of him in front of the kids. Most importantly, he had a lot of time to reflect about all that had happened to him. One thing was evident to him, Sunny Griffith was never going to choose him. In fact, he concluded that she was not the kind person he had thought that she was.

Harold started working on new drawings that included the death of Brenda Johnson. Later that evening, Harold heard his mother shouting at someone on the other end of the phone, she threatened to "put an end to the donations if nothing was done". Moments later, Harold's mother came into his room for the first time in a very long time.

"I called them at school," she said. "I was told you beat up two boys because of a girl."

"That's not true!" Harold shouted back. "Everyone should just leave me alone!"

"It doesn't matter now. You can return to school tomorrow. I've had a talk with your principal."

"Why can't you just leave me alone?" he screamed behind his mother as she left.

The next day at school, everyone kept staring at Harold. He went from the irrelevant kid to the miserable Missouri Monster. Brenda Johnson made sure that name stuck.

"Guess who's back?" one of the kids shouted while Harold was walking through the school hall. "It's the Missouri Monster!" Once again, laughter spread across everywhere at the expense of Harold.

During break that day, while Harold was alone at his table, eating a sandwich, Brenda Johnson came to him.

"So, you're really back," she said "The only thing you've got is your rich family, and that's why you're here. I know that."

Harold's eyes were stationed to his food. He ignored Brenda Johnson and went on eating. "Why not buy your way into getting a date with Sunny, since you're so rich, Monster," she continued. When she realized that Harold was not going to say anything, she lifted the plate before him and poured its content on the floor. She yelled, "Missouri Monster!" as she walked away.

Harold spent the rest of that day in the bathroom crying. He regretted his decision to ask Sunny Griffith out on a date. He hated himself for thinking that even though other kids saw him differently, Sunny would be able to see past what people saw and realize how much he liked her.

Harold cried in his room every day after that, until one Friday night. He felt the urge to do something that would hurt Brenda Johnson. He had already developed an affinity for killing, and though he had several drawings of Brenda's death, he did not know how to organize the kill like they did in the books. So, he came up with a decision to kill the Johnsons' dog. He knew how much Brenda loved the dog. He saw her often on weekends as she walked the Bichon Frise past the Franczyk house.

Since he conceived the thought, Harold's days were occupied with him contemplating how to kill Brenda Johnson's dog and he spent his nights coming up with different variations of the dog's death. He was visibly distracted during classes and teachers noticed it. They informed his mother one day that he was not concentrating in classes and when he got back home that day, his mother asked him about it. She was seated on the brown sofa in the living room, eating an apple. Her cat, Longstaff, was trying to fight for her attention as she talked to Harold.

"Harold?" she said, "Principal Groff called. He said you've been having a hard time concentrating in school." Harold saw that she was drunk. "What is wrong with you, troubled child?"

He ignored her and headed straight to his room. He had never killed anything before, and though he knew what to do, he did not know how to do it. *I could kill Longstaff*, he thought. He needed something to practice with, and his mother's cat was the best idea that occurred to him.

On one of her nights out, Harold killed his mother's cat and buried it. The feeling was not what he had expected. He felt awful and when his mother started looking for the cat, he was filled with regret. His mother searched for Longstaff for days, and when she saw that the cat was gone, she began crying. Some days, she cried for so long and never came out of her room. Harold came back from school one day, and the person he saw was far from his mother. Mrs. Franczyk looked thin and shabby, it scared Harold. He had never seen her in that state before. Harold realized how lonely his mother was and that Longstaff meant more than a pet to her. He wished he had not killed the cat. Afterwards, he discarded his plan to kill Brenda Johnson's dog.

Chapter 4

KHS Connection

"It feels so weird to be back here." Smith was taking in the changes that Kirtland High had gone through since his time there as a student. "I was one of the popular kids, you know. I'm sure you were a nerd in high school."

He laughed as Stapleton raised his eyebrows to the last sentence. "Not exactly a nerd, just a little bit quiet," Stapleton said.

"I bet you were."

"High school wasn't exactly nice for me. After my parents died, I had to work between jobs to fend for myself and my little brother."

Stapleton had never talked about his personal life at all since he started working with him. Smith was surprised and did not know what to say. Stapleton was so cultured, Smith never imagined he grew up under such difficult circumstances. Stapleton always listened to him whenever he talked to him about his own life and family. Sometimes he offered some advice but most times he just listened to him talk. A lot of things made sense now. Stapleton had learned to be responsible for others since he was young.

Maybe that was his own reason for joining the police force, Smith thought.

"I'm so sorry, I didn't know that." Smith uttered slowly.

But Stapleton looked at him and said,

"Cheer up, that was all in the past. Now, what we have to do is find this murderer."

The men found their way towards the principal's office as they attracted the attention of kids that were trying to figure out what a couple of tightly-dressed men were doing within their school halls.

The principal, Mrs. Andrews, was a middle-aged woman. She had the look of someone who was always worried about something. The men introduced themselves and she offered them to sit on the old pair of chairs before her mahogany table. The office looked smaller than Smith could remember, but it carried the smell of old books just as before.

"We need to look into Alice Panabaker's records. Anything the school has on her could prove to be vital in our pursuit for her killer," Smith said.

"We are happy to help in any way we can, gentlemen," she said. "After I got your call, I gathered everything we have about Ms. Panabaker while she was here at Kirtland High School. It is over there on that shelf." Mrs. Andrews stood up and led the men to the shelf located west of the office.

"Thank you, ma'am," Stapleton said.

"I'll be right outside if you need anything," she told the men and left the office.

The detectives spent hours going through everything— bio-data forms, medical records, academic records, but nothing was substantial enough for the men to follow.

"This looks like another dead end," Smith said. He had hoped that they would find at least some kind of a lead. The men both shared the thought that if the person that wanted to kill Alice was from her past in Kirtland, then it was tied to Alice's time here. They had spoken with her parents and everyone they could meet with; they were unable to find anything to follow. Just when he was about to wrap it up, Stapleton noted something.

"It appears Alice was really close with these girls," he said. "They appeared together in several other photos."

Smith dropped the document in his hand and moved closer to check out what his partner was talking about.

"I saw a photo in the Panabakers' house, Alice was with the same set of girls," Smith said. "And that's Sunny Griffith." He pointed to the girl in the middle of the five teenagers in the photos. A new air of enthusiasm moved through the men. If their speculation was true, then one of these girls would know something.

"I think we should have another chat with Sunny Griffith," Smith told his partner and he agreed.

They got the full names of the other three girls with the help of Mrs. Andrews and after they had expressed their gratitude to Mrs. Andrews, they left the school premises.

Back at the precinct, a man was reporting a missing person as the detectives entered. "They said she didn't show up at work." The man looked distressed. "Brenda would never miss today of all days."

Stapleton moved closer to him at the sound of the name and asked, "What is the full name of this person?"

The man turned to him. "Brenda Johnson," he said. Stapleton and Smith shared a look. "She's the lady that anchors the In Kirtland show. You have to believe me, something is wrong. She told me last night that her bosses wanted to remove her from the show, now she's missing."

The officer that the man was previously talking to looked uninterested. Stapleton could understand why. The police got those kinds of reports frequently and most times they turned out to be false alarms. Especially when it was still under twenty-four hours since the person was last seen. After he confirmed that it was the same Brenda Johnson that the man talked about, Stapleton told the officer to take the man's report and send him to his office afterwards.

In his office, the man identified himself as Peter Dawson. He was Brenda's fiancé. They had been engaged for nearly a year. He told them that he was with Brenda at her apartment till a little past eight the previous night. He did not want to leave because she was really worried about work but he had to because he was on a night shift at the hospital where he worked as a lab technician. Very early in the morning, he went to her apartment but he thought she had decided to go to work early. When he called her workplace trying to speak with her to know how it was going with the issue at work, they told him they had not seen her either.

"She was really worried yesterday. I should have stayed with her," he said.

"Was there any sign of a break-in at her apartment?" Smith asked.

"No, there wasn't. The apartment has a rear door by the kitchen. It was locked too. I checked."

Stapleton did not want to reach any conclusion so quickly, but if his instinct was right and Brenda Johnson was truly missing, then there was a connection with the Alice Panabaker's case.

"Mr. Dawson, I'd like you to try other places that you think she might be. We'll see what we can do from here and get back to you," Stapleton said.

Peter Dawson was dismissed and the men talked about the new turn of events. Smith was quick to dismiss Brenda Johnson's connection to Alice Panabaker's case. He rightly based the dismissal on the precedence set by cases of such nature.

"She would probably be somewhere hiding out from them. It happens all the time," he said.

However, Stapleton had other things in mind. To him, there was a strong connection somewhere, call it a veteran's instinct or whatever it is that prompted your actions when you have spent over a dozen years solving homicides. But he also knew that he should not be so quick to jump to conclusions, so he agreed with his partner.

"You're probably right, we'll see," Stapleton said.

Detective Wayne Stapleton could not sleep that night. Something was not right, he knew that. But he had to wait for confirmation that Brenda was really missing. He had earlier checked in with her fiancé and he told him that he had not heard from her yet. Stapleton half-expected a call that would inform him that Brenda Johnson's body was found somewhere. He felt bad for having the thought but he could not help it.

He woke up very early the next morning and headed towards the Gildersleeve Mountains. He walked about the crime scene. He was not sure what he was looking for but he kept looking. He had initially hoped to find Brenda up there, dead. He felt disappointed when he did not. But a greater feeling of guilt overcame him and he decided to let it go. Maybe Brenda Johnson was alive somewhere after all, he concluded. Stapleton stood still suddenly as he heard something move within the woods. He sensed that someone was behind him, watching. He slowly withdrew his gun from his holster and turned around but no one was there.

***

"I could have sworn someone was there with me," Stapleton recounted his experience in the Gildersleeve Mountains to his partner.

"What were you doing there so early anyway?" Smith asked.

"I had a hunch," he said. "So, I decided to check it out."

Smith trusted his partner when it came to matters such as this and he had started to get a feeling himself. "Brenda Johnson hasn't been found yet and it's now been over twenty-four hours. If the cases are connected, then Brenda Johnson might currently be in danger," he said.

"We could launch a search party," Stapleton said.

"We'll need to see Chief Horning if we are to do that," Smith replied.

After the men had revealed to Chief Horning a possible connection between Alice Panabaker's case and the missing Brenda Johnson, the police chief did not hesitate to approve the search. Stapleton suggested that the officers look at locations in Kirtland that are around water bodies. After they had searched for hours, Brenda Johnson's body was eventually found in the Chagrin Spring, head inside water and other parts of her body on dry land, just like Alice Panabaker.

"Exactly like Alice Panabaker," Smith noted. "We can throw away the Melonheads story now."

Stapleton had not said anything since he got the radio call. He was deep in his own thoughts. It all made sense to him now. At least, it was beginning to. Now, they could discard the speculation— one that he was never really inclined towards— that Alice Panabaker was followed to Kirtland. The killer was right there in Kirtland.

And the key to his apprehension hid in whatever the girls were involved in before Alice Panabaker left Kirtland eight years ago. Stapleton thought about that morning. What if it was the killer that came back to the initial crime scene? But why would he do that? he asked himself. He had no answer to that. The killer was steps ahead of him at the moment, but he would catch up soon enough, Stapleton resolved.

Detective Jake Smith caught the sight of his partner. Once again, the man has shown why he was distinguished among the police force. Stapleton had foreseen the connection earlier than he could ever have. Smith was eager to hear the output of his partner's evaluation. It became clear to him now that the same killer was responsible for the two murders. For Chief Horning, a second murder case in a week was the exact opposite of what he wanted for Kirtland. By the time the news would come out, the whole of Kirtland would be thrown into confusion.

Many will fear for their well-being and rightly so, he thought. Only God knows what next this killer had planned for them. Something had to be done, and as it seemed, they had to work as quickly as possible because the killer was obviously moving fast with two kills in a week.

"It couldn't have been that this was a copy-cat, could it?" Officer Bowman, who was among the search party that found the body, asked.

The question caught Stapleton's attention. If it was a copy-cat, then they had a much bigger problem on their hands. But he doubted it. It would have to be that the killers were related in some way for the copy-cat killer to choose Brenda Johnson as the victim. Or it was one hell of a coincidence.

"It could be, but I don't think so," replied Bowman. "We had already established a connection between the victims before today. It is most certainly the same killer."

Stapleton's concern was the media attention that would come with this case, especially now that Brenda Johnson was involved. As if to add to his thoughts,

"The mayor called me about the Alice Panabaker case this morning. He didn't like the media attention it's been bringing." Chief Horning said. "He wants us to wrap it up as fast as possible. But now, this brings a whole new dimension to everything."

The mayor, Paul Griffith, was re-running for a second term. The killings represented bad press for his administration. It could be understood why he wanted things to be wrapped up as quickly as possible.

In Peralta's lab, the detectives, including Chief Horning and Officer Bowman were present as the doctor gave his report. He confirmed that Brenda Johnson was also killed by strangulation. The crime scene was not exactly where he killed her, he had to move the body again, which supported their profile of someone with a significant amount of strength to move a dead body with ease without evidence. Yet again, he informed them that one of the victim's fingers was missing a ring.

"The victim was engaged," Stapleton said. "It was her fiancé that reported that she was missing."

"This one is almost the same as the last one," Dr. Peralta concluded. "I guess it is safe to conclude that you are looking for the same killer."

"What do you mean by almost, doctor?" Stapleton asked.

Dr. Peralta smiled at him and replied, "I thought no one was going to ask. I guess it was always going to be you, Detective Stapleton, huh?" he chuckled in his boyish way. "Okay, before we get distracted," he straightened his coat. "Test results showed that the victim inhaled a significant amount of chloroform before she died. That is, the killer had to render her unconscious."

"So, what does that signify?" It was Smith's turn to ask the question.

"It means that the victim needed to be moved between different locations," Stapleton came in and paused for a second. He appeared to be thinking about his next set of words, as one did if one was about to reveal a big secret. "And the killer didn't want to draw any attention because someone could hear the victim if she was conscious."

"And that's it, Detective!" Dr. Peralta beamed with the pleasure of a teacher who was witnessing a bright student shine.

"If what her fiancé said was true, then Brenda Johnson was at home at night, but we found no sign of any break-in at her apartment," Chief Horning said.

"Maybe she didn't lock her door, but I'll leave that to you gentlemen. After all, you are the detectives." Dr. Peralta winked at Detective Stapleton.

The meeting was dismissed with the chief ordering the detectives to do all they can to catch the psychopath. Everything they needed would be provided to them at full strength.

The two detectives were back again at their board with some kind of clarity, but that came with a new murder case. Though it may not seem so, Stapleton believed that they were edging closer to a breakthrough. It was only a matter of time till they found something. They only needed to dig further into the past of these young women.

"The other names on the girls' list, what do we know about them?" he asked his partner.

"Mary Logan and Elise Mckennie." Smith gave him background information about the girls.

The girls were all members of the cheerleading team when they were at Kirtland High School, he told him. Elise Mckennie was Tony Ardolf's cousin. Tony Ardolf was Paul Griffith's main opposition for the mayoral elections. Apparently, Elise has been so busy helping her cousin with the campaign, they had tried to reach out to her once but she was not able to make time for them. But now that a second murder was on their table, she definitely had to make the time. Contrastingly, Mary Logan recently got out of rehab for serious drug addiction. They had scheduled a meeting with her for the next day. Stapleton still believed that the deaths were connected to something that the five girls were involved in back then. And he was determined to find out what that was. The other girls might potentially be in danger and they had no knowledge of it.

***

Harold went into the large room that used to belong to his father, as he sometimes did when he was really troubled or had a lot on his mind. It made him feel close to his father. The memories of him that he had were close to non-existent. It was so fragile that he sometimes had to look at the photos of him that hung in his room to remind himself how his father looked. Mrs. Franczyk once told her son that he was exactly like his father and that was why he would remain a troubled child like he was. From the day his mother told him that, Harold started taking interest in everything that belonged to his father. He went through the books that he left behind, he read through his journals and studied his lifestyle from everything he was able to get. But one thing Harold had come to learn was that he was nothing like his father. The man was just more reserved than usual. And maybe his unwillingness to communicate made it easy for people— including Harold's mother— to misunderstand him, but he certainly was nothing like the man, he concluded.

He considered himself an outcast. The whole world including his own mother hated him. What he did to deserve such fate was unknown to him. He remembered the last time he was at the grocery store; he saw a girl as he was shopping. He thought she was a cute little girl and decided to say hello. But as he waved to the kid, she yelled at him and screamed for her mother who was not far behind. Harold felt embarrassed by that scene. Even the kid hates me, he thought to himself. He had come to accept his reality as someone that the world generally detested, but what he could not accept was the person he was in high school, the cowardly and scared child that was too weak to fight against oppression and humiliation. He was fighting back now, and it was never going to be enough until he finished the job.

Harold thought he felt better now that he killed Brenda Johnson, much better than Alice Panabaker. He did not have the time to plan out Alice's death and it required a little bit of luck. But he had made detailed drawings of Brenda Johnson's death several months back. It was just as he wanted it. Brenda Johnson made life difficult for him in high school.

Harold allowed his thoughts to wander into the happenings of that day. When he got to Brenda Johnson's apartment and found out that the rear door was unlocked, he could not believe his luck. He watched her for a while, waiting for the right opportunity to attack without raising any alarm. It was hard to fight against the urge to kill her right there in her apartment when she got out of the kitchen. But Harold was aware that if he were to achieve his aim, he had to stick to the plan.

The expression on Brenda Johnson's face was what he had longed for. For several years, Harold had been waiting for that moment when Brenda Johnson would be at his mercy. He took a deep sigh of relief as he strolled out of his father's room. He wondered how people would react now that another person was found dead. Will they still think the Melonheads were responsible? Certainly not, he thought. The police would surely be looking for a real killer now but he was not bothered. Harold believed he was smarter and it felt divine to be tormenting them this day. As Harold left the room, however, one thing that bothered him— even though he would not admit to himself— was his loneliness. He accepted that the world did not want him but he did not want to be alone.

***

The news of Brenda Johnson's murder sent a new wave of panic into Kirtland. Many that had previously put the murder of Alice Panabaker on the Melonheads were left in confusion. People were starting to fear that Kirtland was not a safe place anymore. Everyone from Brenda's workplace was shocked by the news. They had thought that her absence from work was a form of protestation to her removal from the In Kirtland show. Due to the rising popularity of the TV show, Brenda Johnson was well known in Kirtland. It was all that everyone talked about. Her face was all over the papers. The mayor called Chief Horning to ask how it could have happened under his watch. He sounded frustrated when he pleaded with the Chief of Police to do everything possible to stop the killings.

Detectives Jake Smith and Wayne Stapleton visited Brenda Johnson's apartment with her fiancé Peter— who tried to hide his pain as he went with the men. But when he got to her bedroom, he could not suppress it anymore. Tears flowed from Peter Dawson's eyes. He begged the detectives to find the bastard that killed his fiancée. They had told him earlier that Brenda was not wearing her engagement ring when her body was found. They hoped that it would be found in her apartment but it was not there. It made sense to Stapleton because the killer took Alice Panabaker's necklace too. The killer was keeping souvenirs. Nothing looked out of place in the apartment.

"The killer must be very good," Stapleton told his partner. "He was careful to leave no trace behind."

They confirmed that there was no sign of a break-in. Brenda's aged neighbor told the men that she heard someone leave the apartment twice that night. She was not exactly sure when but the second time was quite late. She was about to go to bed at that time.

The detectives speculated that the first one that she heard was Peter Dawson leaving the apartment and the second would be the killer, carrying an unconscious

Brenda away from the apartment. But what they still did not understand was how the killer got in and how he carried her all the way to the Chagrin Spring. Brenda's neighbor told them that she did not hear any sound of a vehicle.

"He must have parked elsewhere," Smith noted.

With everything they had, they built up a profile. They presumed that the killer was a male with a well-built physique that made him physically capable of moving the victims with ease. Also, he had a means of transportation. That meant that they were looking for a vehicle that was around the area late that night. They asked around, but no one seemed to notice anything. Just like when they asked around in Greater Lakes Mall, no one was able to provide any information apart from the woman from the temple that came to report that she saw her. The detectives left the apartment and went back to the KPD building where they decided to visit Mary Logan's apartment.

Chapter 5

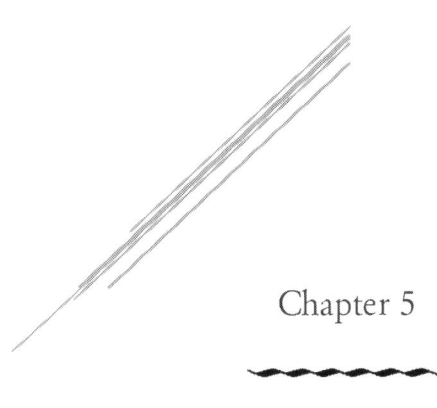

The Suspect

Detective Smith knocked on the old, grey, wooden door at Mary Logan's apartment. It reminded him of his childhood. He was not exactly sure why, but the door scratched open a portion of his childhood memories. It was the time he spent at his grandfather's house one summer. It was where he first saw a firearm up close. The old man had served in the military and lost a limb in action. Perhaps, that summer was why he joined the police force. He had never thought about it that way.

"No one is answering," Smith said. The house sat somewhere off the road along Maple Street, isolated. "Guess she is not home then. We'll have to come back later," Stapleton concluded.

"What do you want?"

The detectives turned their heads at the sound of the voice. They could not hide their amazement when they saw that it was a woman's. It was deep, and could easily have passed for a grown man's voice.

"We're from the Kirtland Police Department. We are looking for Mary Logan," Smith said.

"I'm Mary Logan. Sorry, I got your notice. Please come in."

She led the men into the house. It really did look like his grandfather's house, Smith thought again, examining the interior. Mary offered the men seats on the pastel green couch in the small living room.

"I know this is about Alice and Brenda," she said. "What I don't understand is why you wanna talk to me. We haven't been friends since high school." She seemed impatient.

"Yes, you are right," Stapleton told her. "It is about their murder. We're just trying to look for some information and we'd like you to answer some questions."

She nodded.

"We learned that you were close friends with both of them in high school, including Sunny Griffith and Elise

Mckennie."

"Yes, but I guess we weren't friends after all."

"Why would you say that?" Staple pressed.

"I'm sorry, I know we are talking about murder but I just can't sit here with you guys and act like I care about these people. Not after everything I have gone through."

Stapleton looked at his partner, he knew Smith very well. Words like that could make him consider Mary a suspect. Especially with the knowledge of her history with drugs.

"Tell us more about it, Ms. Logan," Stapleton said.

"The five of us were truly close in high school," she started. "And there was this guy on the football team, Jackson Hayes. Sunny started dating him during our junior year. I heard they got engaged recently."

She told them about how she was actually the one that Jackson noticed first, but because Sunny was an orphan, the group let her have a way with a lot of things.

"Though I'm not an orphan, my parents were never there for me either," she said "My dad left when I was a kid and my mom has been a mess since."

She revealed that even after Jackson and Sunny started dating, Jackson still came to her. They went on seeing each other in secret. She admitted that she should have stopped it when she could, but she was so naive and she thought that they had something special together. By the end of high school, before Alice left, Mary got pregnant and she told Brenda Johnson about it. Brenda was the only one who knew that she was seeing Jackson. Brenda told the rest of them except Sunny, and the girls agreed that it was best if Sunny did not know about it.

"That was how we shielded her away from everything because she had no parents," Mary pointed out.

She continued. Elise told them that she knew a place where they removed babies for an amount. It was illegal but they had no choice, she said. After all, Sunny must not be aware. The girls contributed the money for the abortion but she could not go through with it. She was scared, she was barely eighteen years old. When the girls saw that she was really not going to get rid of the pregnancy, they left her alone. But it had to be kept a secret from Sunny, they told her. After Alice left, they all forgot about her, except Sunny. She would visit her in the mobile home where she hid herself, malnourished and depressed. Sometimes Sunny brought food for her. Sunny would ask her who was responsible for the baby but she did not want to get between Jackson and her. So, she lied that the person left and she did not want to talk about it. Soon after, around the time she was about to give birth, Sunny left for college. The baby died at birth and the experience affected her so much that she turned to drugs—heroine especially. Her life had been miserable since then and even when they all came back, none of the girls reached out to her except Sunny. After she got into rehab, she heard that Sunny and Jackson Hayes were back together again.

"And when I got out, I reached out to Brenda and Elise. At least there was no baby, maybe we could tell them what happened. But none of them wanted to have anything to do with a drug addict." Tears were flowing down her cheeks but her voice was still steady. It occurred to Stapleton that she was used to crying. She must have cried so much in the past that it did not matter to her anymore.

"I could not bear seeing Sunny trying to act nice to me, so I told her not to come to me anymore. So, I'm sure you could understand why I don't want to have anything to do with them. I was shocked to hear about it, but unfortunately, I can't help you here, detectives."

"We understand, Ms. Logan," Stapleton said. "Thank you for your time and I'm really sorry about everything." Stapleton had more to say. He wanted to tell her that she should tell Sunny the truth because sooner or later, it would come out. And since Sunny was the only one that cared about her, she deserved to know the truth. But he was just a homicide detective, not Mary Logan's therapist. It was not in his job description to give unsolicited advice.

While Mary Logan sat before them the whole time, telling her story, Smith kept thinking about how Mary Logan had the motive for the murders. He understood that she had gone through a lot, more than anyone that age should ever have to but he could not help but shake the feeling away. He said nothing as they stood up to bid Mary Logan farewell.

"Thank you once again, Ms. Logan," Stapleton told her. "But you have to know that even though I understand your position in this, this is an ongoing investigation and if there is a need to have a chat with you, we will have to do this again."

She nodded and the men left the house.

On their way back to the precinct, Smith decided to declare his mind to his partner behind the wheel. "Mary Logan checks all the boxes; she has a motive. It fits perfectly well," Smith said.

"Why did it take you so long? Been waiting for you to say this as soon as we left the lady's house," Stapleton said to his partner, smiling. "Okay, given her history and circumstances, she has the motive. But that's where it all ends; those women were killed by someone who knew what he was doing. The killings were well staged, and Mary Logan doesn't look like someone who could pull that off to me. Besides, she doesn't fit our profile."

"Well, it's possible that she has an accomplice. Look at her, she did not care about the deaths of her friends!"

"Okay, I'm not ruling anything out. But even if what you're saying is true, we still need more evidence." Stapleton told him.

He understood what Mary Logan had gone through, having no parents around. After his own parents died, Stapleton— alongside his younger brother— became exposed to hardship. It was hard enough to get something to eat and he had to feed his brother as well. They both could not continue school at that point. He worked between different menial jobs to provide for both of them. At a point when things became too difficult, he began drinking. He hid the bottles from his brother because he did not want him taking up a drinking habit as well. But when he saw that he was unsuccessful in his attempt to not influence his younger brother, he stopped drinking. Stapleton was lucky to meet a man that took him in as a laundry boy. The man paid for their education while he worked for him. If he had not met him, he certainly was not going to turn out as he did. Smith on the other hand came from a place of privilege. *Maybe that's why he could not identify with Mary Logan like he did,* Stapleton thought. To Smith, it was either black or white.

The men decided that they needed to have a proper chat with Sunny Griffith. The mayor's office was just beside the KPD building. They met Sunny outside the office's building, by the payphone. She appeared to have just gotten off the phone.

"Hello again, Ms. Griffith," Smith greeted.

"Gentlemen," she returned. "I've been expecting you since the news of Brenda's murder. I just got off the phone with Elise Mckennie. In the space of one week, two of our friends were murdered, I'm not sure what to think."

"That is why we have come to see you. We were just coming from your friend Mary's place," Stapleton said.

"Mary? How is she?"

"She's hanging in there. Ms. Griffith, where can we sit down to talk?" Stapleton asked.

She led them inside to an empty office.

"You have to know that we think that the same killer killed them both. The killer staged the murders in a very specific way," Stapleton told her. "If there's anything you are holding back from us it's time you told us, because we think they were both targeted."

"Does that mean I might be in danger?" Sunny asked with a hint of fear.

"Well, we don't have enough information to arrive at that conclusion yet. That is why we need your help to establish a connection," Stapleton said.

"I've been doing a lot of thinking too but it's all confusing. Alice left this town years ago."

"We think it has to do with your time together in high school," Smith said.

"I'm not sure if I should say this but Alice and Brenda had a fight in high school," she said. "Alice slept with Brenda's boyfriend, Tyron Baker. He is the first son of the owner of Baker Constructions. It was a big fight and Brenda was not talking to Alice for weeks. Tyron said he was drunk and he accused Alice of taking advantage of him," she stopped for a moment. "I don't know if what I'm saying is relevant, I just can't think of anything else."

"Please continue, Ms. Griffith," Stapleton said.

"Okay, so after the whole thing, Alice and Brenda got back to talking but Brenda did not go back to Tyron. I don't know how she did it but Alice was able to convince Brenda that Tyron was lying. We were just really happy to see them back together. I didn't know if it was the truth or not. My fiancé Jackson was Tyron's closest friend back then, he told me that Tyron was really hurt by what Alice did." Sunny Griffith stopped again, looked down at her feet, then lifted her head and said, "I still don't think that would make Tyron want to... ," She was looking at Stapleton, trying to know what he thought. "After all, it was years ago. I'm really confused, detectives."

Smith gave Stapleton a knowing look. The murders have opened up a lot of teenage secrets that could potentially affect their current lives, even after all those years. Stapleton was sure that more of those secrets had died with Alice Panabaker and Brenda Johnson. But could Tyron Baker have decided to kill the two women because of a scandal from their teenage years? If he did, why wait till now. In Tyron Baker, Stapleton supposed that they had someone who fitted the profile and had the resources to have committed the murder. But everything looked to be on a thin sheet of paper. They would need to speak with Tyron Baker first.

"Ms. Griffith, thank you for your time. If there's anything that comes to your mind, please reach out to us," Stapleton told her.

"Okay. I'll do that."

When the men were about to leave, Smith turned back. "Could you get us an appointment with Elise Mckennie? We have been trying to get a minute with her but apparently she's been too busy."

"The mayor's birthday is tomorrow. He'll be having a party in his house and I'm sure she will be there with Tony Ardolf. It is more of a Kirtland public function than a birthday party. I'll make sure you get to have a chat with her."

"Thank you for your help, Ms. Griffith. We'll be there tomorrow," Smith said and the men left.

It was eleven in the morning. Detectives Jake Smith and Wayne Stapleton were inside the Baker Construction building. They had been directed by a woman to the building that had ENGINEERING written boldly on its foreside. She said Tyron Baker would be somewhere in the building. They approached a man and introduced themselves to him. He had a white helmet on, and when they told him they were from the KPD, he tightened up. He left them to get Tyron Baker.

"Morning, officers." Tyron greeted.

"Detectives, actually. Detective Smith and," pointing to his partner, "Detective Stapleton from the Kirtland Police Department." Smith would not let it go, not for Tyron Baker. He expected better. Stapleton had to suppress a smile at his partner's reaction.

"Oh, I apologize for that, detectives," he laughed too hastily.

Tyron Baker fits the profile, Stapleton thought. He was about a couple of inches taller than him. He looks fit, and he certainly would be able to carry an average-weight woman.

"We'd like to speak with you about the murder of Alice Panabaker and Brenda Johnson," Smith said. "We understand that you knew them when they were alive."

"Yes, I did. Especially Brenda Johnson, we kind of dated in high school. But Alice left Kirtland long ago. can't even remember the last time I saw her."

"We think the murders are connected and have to do with the time you spent together in high school."

"I'm confused. You think someone from Kirtland High killed them?"

"As you said earlier," Stapleton said. "Alice left Kirtland right after she graduated from high school. We thought that you might be able to help with answering a few questions."

"I already told you, I don't know anything about Alice. I dated Brenda for a while, and that didn't work out. That's it." Tyron was getting impatient. He was obviously hiding something. The detectives wanted to make sure that the scandal with Alice was the only thing he was hiding.

Smith moved closer to Tyron Baker. He began in a low, stern voice, "We've had a chat with Sunny Griffith and we already know why Brenda broke up with you. So, for your own sake, don't hide anything from us."

Tyron Baker was hit by surprise and his reaction gave him up. But what the detectives were interested in was if he was hiding something else.

"I'm not sure what you want me to say. Okay, I cheated on Brenda with Alice Panabaker," he sniffed. "Now they are both dead and you think I killed them, is that it?"

"You tell us what to think," Stapleton said.

"I think I'm gonna need my lawyer before I say anything else."

Tyron summoned his father and the detectives had to leave him alone, for now.

As the men drove on, Smith said to his partner, "He certainly looked the part. And for a second, it was as if he was hiding something we still don't know about."

Stapleton agreed with his partner. It appeared that Tyron Baker was hiding something other than what Sunny already told them. Whatever it was that he was trying to hide, Stapleton was sure it had to do with Alice

Panabaker and he certainly would make sure that he got it out of him. Now, it was about time they spoke with Elise Mckennie. If there was anything she knew, they had to know it too.

"You ready for the party tonight, Jake?"

"I sure am. I'm picking up my suit from the laundry later."

"Maybe you should bring Maureen along but who will stay with the kids?" Stapleton teased.

The two men burst into laughter.

***

At around half past seven in the evening, Detective Stapleton joined his partner in the mayor's house. It took him a while to identify him among the crowd. The large hall where the party was held was lit with gold string lights. It had been a long time since Stapleton last attended a party. He thought it looked glorious, with everyone glowing in the lights. He scanned around, looking for his partner. He noticed many smiling faces, mostly women, and a few business-looking faces that seemed too eager to put the party behind them as quickly as possible. He saw Sunny Griffith moving from a group to another, exchanging pleasantries, hugging, shaking hands. Finally, he saw Smith, like most of the men present— including himself— he wore a black suit. His black bow tie sat elegantly atop the collar of his crisp white shirt as the light bathed his tanned skin in bright gold. Anyone that could see would know that he was waiting for something. Not interested in entering the crowd, Stapleton waved until Smith could see him.

"You look good, Wayne," Smith said as he approached him. "You should dress up more often."

They both laughed. It took just a moment and the men were back in business again.

"I spotted Sunny Griffith as I entered. Have you seen any sign of Elise Mckennie?" Stapleton asked.

"Not yet, but Tyron Baker is here."

"What is he doing here?"

"It's not unusual, Baker Constructions have some government projects in their hands."

"Maybe he'll be relaxed enough to talk. But I doubt it after the scene from yesterday."

The detectives turned their heads as they heard sudden rumbling voices behind them. Tony Adolf just came in, and he was being greeted by the people around the hall entrance. He was bald, of average height and his suit was striped. Stapleton found it funny that the man could come to his rival's birthday and attempt to steal the show.

"I better go fetch Sunny," Smith said.

"I'll be right here," Stapleton informed his partner as he left.

Stapleton looked around him. He did not think he would ever be able to fit into this kind of world. The fake smiles and dramatized greetings were not just for him. It felt odd to stand there among them like he was one of them. When he saw Smith earlier, he blended in easily like he was one of them. He simply could not. Stapleton saw a man standing not too far from him, he looked uncomfortable too. *Maybe I'm not alone after all*, he thought. He moved closer.

"You look tense, I guess this isn't your crowd either."

The man turned to him. He saw that he was much younger.

"I'm not really sure what I'm doing here," he said, smiling nervously. "My mother used to get these invites before she died. I guess they just sent it out just the same."

"Oh, I'm sorry about your mom. That still doesn't explain why you are here," Staple pointed out.

For a man with such build, his voice sounded soft, almost like a child's. "I wanted to check it out. Actually, I haven't been to a lot of cocktail parties," he said.

It was clear to Stapleton that he had not been to any party at all. He was surprised. If his mother was a permanent name on the RSVP list, then he must have come from a rich family.

"Nice. Wayne Stapleton." Stapleton introduced himself, extending his hand.

"Franczyk, Harold Franczyk."

"Nice to meet you. I hope you get to attend more of this," Stapleton shared a laugh with him. "Oh, I have to go. Enjoy, Harold." Stapleton said quickly as he saw Smith and Sunny, navigating their way to him.

The mayor called the attention of everyone. He wanted to make an announcement. He was flanked on either side by his wife and daughter.

"Thank you all for coming here today. It would have been a perfect night if not for the recent killings that hang over Kirtland. Nevertheless, we must continue to stay strong as we walk through these dark hours together as one. I want to introduce my beloved family, my wife, my daughter, and my ever-efficient niece, Sunny Griffith." Cheers rose among the crowds at the mention of Sunny. "God bless you all and God bless this city of faith and beauty. Enjoy your night."

Applauds followed and everyone continued with the party.

Outside the house with Elise Mckennie and Sunny Griffith, the detectives thanked Sunny for helping them. She was about to leave when Tyron Baker appeared before them, a little bit drunk.

"How could you accuse me of killing Alice and Brenda?" He faced Sunny. "Just because I cheated on Brenda, does that make me a killer? Answer me!"

Sunny was left speechless. She helplessly looked at the detectives, waiting for them to come to her rescue.

"No one accused you of killing them. We were only looking for answers that we hoped you could provide," Smith said.

"No, don't patronize me. I know how this works! You all but said I killed them. And to you Sunny, you think you are better because you have Jackson, right? Well, let me tell you this, Jackson cheated on you with

Mary Logan too. It has always been Mary Logan before you. He reached out to her after she got out of rehab." Jackson Hayes came out just in time to hear that part.

"Ask him yourself if you think I'm lying," Tyron said.

"What are you talking about, man?" Jackson Hayes said. "Shut the hell up."

Sunny could not believe her ears. She faced Jackson, "Jackson, tell me he's lying." Jackson bowed down his head in shame. "So, it's true," she bit her lower lip as tears rolled down her cheeks. "You liar!" At that moment, everything began to make sense to Sunny. "Tell me, was the baby yours?" she asked.

"What baby? I don't know what you are talking about, Sunny." Jackson was confused.

"Yes, it was his," Elise Mckennie spoke. Everything was out anyway. "But Mary didn't tell him. We all agreed to keep it from you both. It's a long story, Sunny."

"What are you talking about, Elise?!" Jackson yelled.

Elise explained everything to them. When she told them that they thought they were only protecting her, Sunny screamed, "Nobody asked for your protection!" and when Elise said that they did not want to break what she had with Jackson, she shot her out with, "It's all lies!"

Jackson Hayes left the group first, he was too confused to say anything. Why did Mary not tell him anything? He recently contacted her. All he wanted to do was make sure she was getting better. He had always loved Mary Logan. But with Sunny, he had perfection, and that was why he chose Sunny.

Sunny realized that everything she thought she knew was painted with lies. How could she have been so foolish? It was all before her. Anytime she brought it up with Mary, she would tell her that the baby's father left and she did not want to talk about it. How painful it must have been for her, she thought.

The murder of Alice Panabaker and Brenda Johnson dug out the deepest of holes, Stapleton accounted on his way home. And as it seemed, there were many more to come. Which begged the question, who murdered Alice Panabaker and Brenda Johnson?

Chapter 6

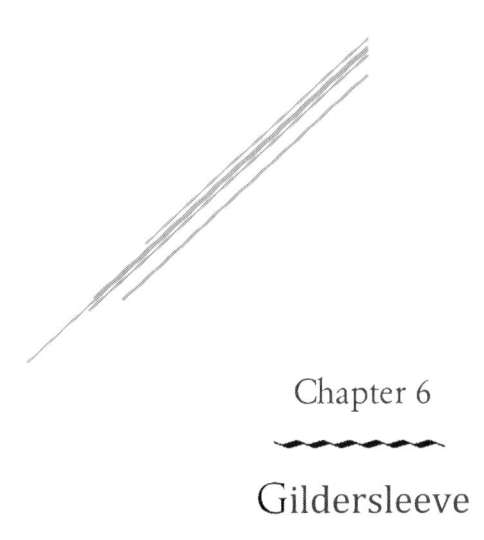

Gildersleeve

In his usual manner, Stapleton leaned against the large oak table in his office, narrowing his eyes on the board before him. His cadet blue shirt, with two buttons undone, clung tightly to his body in the embrace of the chill autumn air. His brown hair, still a little damp, curled sideways in a military style. Though he never served in the military, he was a man that had the utmost respect for the military. If it were not for his brother, whom he did not want to leave behind, he would have served when the opportunity came.

Twelve years and counting as a homicide detective, Stapleton had grown accustomed to dealing with unforeseen changes in the circumstances that tied to a case. It had become habitual that when on a case, he found himself strongly anticipating a certain twist; a flip in the course of the case that was always bound to happen. For Stapleton, that brought clarity. It came with the unexpected, and he had cultured himself to prepare for it.

But it was different this time, even though a lot turned out to be not what it seemed, especially after that night at the mayor's party, that did not make this case less puzzling. In fact, Stapleton was no less confused as that cold morning when he first saw Alice Panabaker's body in the Gildersleeve Mountains. They have two murders already on their hands, yet they had nothing close to a suspect. What they had was a group of friends, or supposed friends, who had made some regrettable mistakes as teenagers.

The killer was smart, Stapleton had to give that to him. He had never encountered a case where the killer was so organized and meticulous. Almost professional. Except that he found no clue— though not for the want of trying— that suggested why a professional hit man would target two young ladies from Kirtland. Besides, the disturbing manner by which the victims were staged showed that there was a personal affair to this case. Which led all the way back to Kirtland High School.

Most days, Stapleton was as sure as a gun that it all had something to do with the school, but some days like this, he did not know what to think. After all he had learned about the two victims so far, he had not been able to figure out where the connection to someone so sophisticated in his thinking and execution lay.

It appeared that the killer was a perfectionist. He took time to cover his tracks. He must possess a painstaking attention to detail. This discernment troubled Stapleton. He felt irritated as he realized that he was almost admiring the unknown killer, or at least his approach to work. He turned around and stretched his long arms over the table, reaching for a pack of cigarettes. He needed to get himself off his current mood. He cursed under his breath as the pack fell off to the opposite side of the table. He went round the table to pick it up. His Grandon boots made a knocking sound as he walked. It was early and he was just about the only person in that part of the KPD building.

He lit up the cigarette. He had not smoked in a while and the pack actually belonged to his partner. He returned to his previous thoughts as he started smoking. He had always been able to catch these psychopaths at their games. He was famously known among his colleagues to be able to accurately think exactly like the killers in his cases, an attribute which would eventually lead to their apprehension.

If you choose being a homicide detective as your profession; then you should be prepared to deal with psychopaths of different kinds. For sure, Stapleton had encountered his own fair share of psychopaths. From a husband who killed his pregnant wife because he believed he was not the father, to another that took the bold step to murder his wife, together with their neighbor because he thought they were having an affair behind his back, or a young disturbed man who kidnapped high school girls and raped them before killing them off. Definitely, he was not a stranger to the world of people like that.

He held a silver pen, which he spun continuously. The pen was the only thing left he had of his father. He had never written with it, not once. But the pen had helped him through the darkest hours of his life. After their parents died, life became impossible to live for Stapleton and his brother. Sometimes, he became too scared from thinking about how they could end up— dead from severe hunger. But whenever he twirled the pen like he did now, he felt close to his father. It felt like his father was there with him as he fought the battle of survival, for the both of them.

It got him through the hungry, cold nights in the small cell he was locked in when he was caught stealing bread from a retailer. He was fifteen. They had gone without tasting food for days, and his brother had started to look sick and lifeless. When Stapleton saw that his hands had begun shaking, he went to the market. He thought he could steal a loaf of bread and give both himself and his brother a break from the aching state of gnawing hunger. The retailer had caught him while he tried to snatch the loaf off her tray. The tall, hairy, pink-faced woman had screamed so much that Stapleton became too frightened to move. She dragged him to the police and he was thrown in a cell that had two other men.

He held the pen through the two scary nights he spent there, spinning it while he thought of his brother that lay hungry in the abandoned train station they lived in. Before he was released, he took the beating of his life. He still recalled how he had felt from the agonizing lashes from the whipping. Even after those years of hardship, he kept the pen and developed a habit of spinning it around his fingers when he found himself against a difficult situation like this. Some days, he thought about his parents and wished they could see how he and his brother— who is now a practicing doctor in Cleveland— turned out.

"It's barely six, Wayne!" Detective Jake Smith was surprised to meet his partner as he came in. He walked towards the board, trying to check out what Stapleton was studying so hard that made him oblivious to the door behind him. "Morning, man." Smith said as he patted him briefly on the shoulder.

"I couldn't sleep," Stapleton turned to him. "I kept thinking about the case." He did not expect to see him so soon. He looked as if he needed to sleep.

Smith understood his partner. He was aware of Stapleton's relentless attitude toward his job. He always had to get to the root of any case. In Stapleton's world, no case was unsolvable. But Smith had begun to fear for the sake of his partner that this one might be different. It's been a full week since Brenda Johnson's murder and it was becoming clear that if it ended with her, they might not be able to unravel the truth about the killings and the killer would walk free. He knew Stapleton could not accept this and that was what he dreaded.

As though he could read his mind, Stapleton turned to him and said, "Whoever killed these women, can't just be allowed to get away with it." He was dramatic with the way he talked. He paused, as if he wanted to say more but was looking for the best way to put it out to his partner. "There's gotta be something, something we can follow, uh? We just have to dig deeper and... ." He paused. Stapleton saw that he did not share his enthusiasm. He must be thinking he was getting obsessed with the case.

Smith knew he had caught him, so he said quickly, "Maybe, uh... maybe we should expand our list." He turned his face away and rubbed it down to the chin before he turned back to Stapleton. "There might be others from the school we haven't checked."

Stapleton did not like to be patronized that way, but he would let this one pass. Besides, Smith was right, the only thing that tied the two victims was Kirtland High and if their time together in the school had something to do with their murders, then there was something they were still missing. He had initially thought that Smith's reason for showing up so early to work was the same as his, but judging by their earlier exchange, that clearly was not the case. So, why did Smith come in so early?

"Why are you here so early?" Stapleton shot at him. His face, relaxed and expressionless.

Smith was visibly affected by the question, he had initially thought about what to say to Stapleton when he saw him earlier. But since he started with the case, he thought he was not going to bring the matter up anymore. How was he going to explain to his partner that it was to get away from his wife and that he had been coming in early like this for the past couple of months?

"Um... I just... ." Smith looked helplessly at his partner and when he saw that he had to tell him something, he gave up. "It's my marriage, alright. I don't enjoy my home anymore, so I come here every morning as early as possible to get away from it."

Smith could not interpret the expression on Stapleton's face but he certainly did not look surprised. He felt embarrassed for having to talk about himself like that.

"I can't say I'm surprised," Stapleton said, after they had both stayed in silence for a brief moment. "I mean, I knew something was going on between you and Maureen but I didn't know it was this serious."

"I don't know, Wayne. We just can't seem to spend a minute together without arguing about one thing or the other and it'd started to look awkward in front of the kids so I thought if I spent less time at home with her, they won't have to see all that crap." Smith let out a distressed sigh.

"Jake, I'm sure the both of you can get through this. And I also think you should talk to her, rather than hide here all day."

"We don't even talk anymore." Smith raised his hands and dropped them in frustration.

"I really think you should talk to her."

***

A few hours into the day, Tyron Baker walked into the Kirtland Police Department. The detectives did not expect to see him after what happened that night at the party. Stapleton saw him first, as he spoke to a uniformed officer in the central office of the KPD. By the way he dressed, Stapleton knew he came there from work. He was eager to know why Tyron Baker would take a quick break from work to visit them at the precinct. If their previous meetings were anything to go by, he clearly showed that he did not want anything to do with the cops. Stapleton walked over to the men.

"I'll take it from here, Officer."

"Detective!" Tyron jumped.

If he had come to see the detectives, he certainly did not act like it. The beads of sweats on his face made him look older than he really was. Stapleton stood directly in front of him, Tyron saw that he was half a head taller. He was intimidated by his figure and he tried so much to conceal it. Stapleton noticed the flesh of mud that stuck out beneath his brown boots and the greasy stain on his grey t-shirt.

"What are you doing here?"

"Um... I... I'm here to talk to you."

He was hesitating, he was beginning to realize that coming there might have been a huge mistake. He stared nervously around the crowded office. Someone might recognize him. Tyron Baker of the Baker Constructions in a police station could potentially end up being a PR issue for the company. His father had specifically warned him to stay off the case and if this blew up on him, he would never forgive him for it. Stapleton got his clue and he directed him into their office, where they joined Detective Smith.

"What's daddy's little boy doing here?" he said as soon as Tyron walked into the office. Tyron was pissed off and that was what he wanted. Smith still harbored some contempt toward him because of the way he dealt with them the last time.

"He claims he has things to say." Stapleton could sense the tension between the men but he would rather solve this case than tend to their ego. "Please sit down, Mr. Baker." He offered him a seat in one of the single visitor's chairs that had KPD inscribed on them.

"Got a change of mind, uh? Can't sleep because of your conscience?" Smith blurted out again.

That was it for Tyron, he had decided to come to them at his own will and he was not going to be dragged for that. He jerked himself off the seat. Stapleton shot his partner a quick glance. He expected a professional conduct from him regardless of how Tyron had behaved in the past.

"I suggest we keep our cool and remember why we are all here today— to find the person that killed these ladies and took them away from their families," Stapleton gestured with his hand as he talked the men down. Tyron returned to his seat. "Mr. Baker, please do continue."

The detectives decided to stay on their feet. With folded arms, they were waiting to hear what he had to say. Smith was becoming impatient as Tyron stalled. He was few seconds away from yelling at him when he finally spoke, "Detective Smith was not wrong, I need to clear my conscience. I don't feel comfortable keeping all the information I have to myself, knowing that I could probably help you guys to catch the real killer." He ran his hand through his head and looked up. "I know I acted like a jerk the other day." He spoke slowly, without looking at the men. "I was just so upset about Alice's murder, not that I'm happy about Brenda's but Alice and I had something special. Brenda was all about superficial things but Alice was different." His eyes became heavy with unshed tears.

He sniffed and continued, "My parents had a big fight in my senior year. It was so serious that my dad moved out of the house. It really got to me. Alice noticed my withdrawn attitude and she helped me through it all. She even helped to get my grades up." He paused for a while, looked up to the men and continued, "I was dating Brenda at that time but Alice and I got intimate and the news came out somehow. After that, things ended really badly between us. I made some mistakes, too."

"Yeah, I think we got a piece of that from Sunny," Smith said. "Is that all you came here to tell us, Mr. Baker?"

"I'm sure he has something important to tell us." Stapleton kept his eyes on Tyron Baker while he spoke. "Is that not true, Mr. Baker?"

Tyron got on his feet and started pacing around the office. Smith was about to say something when Stapleton made a gesture for him to hold on.

"Alright, I know what this is gonna look like," he finally stopped and said to the men. "But you gotta understand that I loved Alice so much. I would never do anything to hurt her."

Stapleton could see that his partner, with the expression on his face as he turned to him, thought Tyron Baker was crazy. But Stapleton knew Tyron Baker was about to reveal something and if he had slept on that decision before coming to them, he would have decided against it. Now that he was here, Stapleton was going to make sure he got whatever it was that Tyron Baker had to say out of him, so he asked him in a stern tone, "Tell us exactly what happened, Mr. Baker."

Tyron went back to the chair and took a deep breath before he sat down. He tried to calm himself as he placed his hands on the table before him. He locked his fingers together and started with a low voice, "After Alice left Kirtland, I realized how much I was in love with her. All attempts to get in touch with her were unsuccessful but I kept trying, even after college. Three years ago, she replied to one of my letters. I was happy at first, until I read the content of the letter. She was still angry about what I did and she said," Tyron paused, trying to hold back the tears that were now rolling down his left cheek, "she said she hoped she never had to set her eyes on me again. But I realized that," Tyron brought out a brown envelope from his pocket and passed it to Stapleton, "I realized that she was not happy in Pittsburgh, so I wanted to make things right between us, at least." Tyron paused. He waited for Stapleton to go through the letter.

Stapleton passed the letter to his partner after he had gone through it, "So, what did you do?" he asked.

Tyron Baker recounted his quest to find Alice Panabaker in Pittsburgh, which was successful, thanks to the postal address on the letter. However, his meeting with Alice did not end well. She dismissed him and also warned him against future visitations.

"Since Alice made it clear in the letter that she was never coming back to Kirtland," he continued, "I was really shocked to see her on Halloween. She was entering the forest around Gildersleeve when I saw her. We had just concluded a survey around the area." Tyron looked up to the detectives. He believed he was now officially a suspect with what he was revealing, especially with the way he had withheld the information.

"I know what this looks like, but believe me, detectives, I would never hurt Alice."

"Tell us what happened, Mr. Baker," Stapleton pressed.

Tyron gulped and wiped off the dots of sweat on his face. "I followed her into the forest, and we got into an argument." He stopped and stared blankly past the men. "I didn't even know she smoked." Tyron pointed to a spot on his neck. "She did this to me with a cigarette. I pushed her out of reflex but she was okay when I left her there in the woods."

He looked at the men again, looking for any expression that would show their stand concerning his innocence. He found none. Not even from Smith that openly resented him. So, he continued, "But what caught my attention as I left the woods was the truck that was parked on the other side of the road. It was an old, not worn-out model. I thought it was really nice. It was just parked there. It looked out of place but then it was Halloween, people are weird on Halloween," he paused again. This time he was looking for the right words to say.

"I think if Alice was killed around the same time I was there, the truck might belong to the killer." After he had said the words, he realized he was speaking to real-life detectives so he added, "I'm probably wrong. I just wanted to tell you everything I know and that's just about it."

Smith, who had earlier retreated to a corner, started walking toward him. "And you didn't think to come forward with this information earlier?"

Stapleton intercepted his partner and pushed his back, "Back off, Smith!"

"I didn't know how. I don't want to be charged with a murder I didn't commit." He turned to Stapleton, "Please understand that I was only scared. I'm sorry."

"What was the color of the truck?" Stapleton asked him. He was doing everything to suppress his own anger. He still could not believe that Tyron Baker kept this information from them, even after they had gone to him looking for some. If he wanted to have his way, he would lock him up in a holding cell right away.

"Blue, the type of blue that could have easily been grey," Tyron replied. Now that he had said everything he felt better. Surprisingly to himself, he was not bothered about the men's feelings toward him. All he cared about was the fact that he had said everything he had to say. Period. "Sorry, I'm bad with colors but I would recognize that beauty any day."

Stapleton knew that if Tyron Baker was the killer, he would not have come to them. At least not with that amount of detail, but he had to make sure of that first. Tyron Baker was allowed to go, but he was told not to leave Kirtland and that he could be summoned anytime.

He agreed and told them he was ready to help them to find Alice's killer.

Stapleton put a tail on him, the officer was to report to them daily. If there was anything Tyron Baker was up to, Stapleton was going to make sure he lost at his own game. However, if the true killer was still out there— as he strongly suspected— the killer might have spotted Tyron with Alice in the woods.

***

As Harold zipped up his leather jacket, thoughts of Sunny flashed through his mind, yet again. Since that night at the mayor's house, he had found it difficult to get Sunny out of his mind. When he saw her smooth face that night, Harold felt something tighten within him. She had to be the most beautiful person on earth. He recalled the way her hair moved slowly as she walked elegantly from one group to another, exchanging pleasantries. If he were to be honest with himself, Sunny Griffith was exactly why he decided to attend the party. When the mail arrived with the invitation to the mayor's party, his heart jumped at the thought of seeing Sunny. He could not have rejected the chance.

Harold slipped his feet into his father's boots, one after the other. The bluish-gray footwear was one of his favorites among all that his father left behind. His favorite was the pocket knife. He examined the antique knife for a brief moment before he pushed it into his pocket. He walked toward the window. He had picked this room over his father's because of the view. It was most exquisite during fall like this. He could see the Kirtland Temple from there and the maple-beech forest to the east of the temple. The bright yellow foliage complemented the white building to create a stunning view.

His mind wandered once more to the events that took place at the party. When he saw the lot of familiar faces flooding out one after the other, Harold had instantly decided to see what was going on. He hid behind an empty stable and heard everything that was said that night. A possibility occurred to him, one which he was all too eager to shake away. Since Jackson Hayes and Sunny will surely be separated now after everything that was revealed that night, he had the opportunity to get closer to Sunny. He was definitely not the same boy from high school, Harold thought to himself. One other thing that Harold found out that night was that the man that had walked up to him earlier during the party, Wayne Stapleton, was the lead detective on the cases. He seemed like a decent man to him, but he decided it was best he stood clear of him. It was ten at night when Harold made his way toward Mary Logan's house.

The drive to her house took Harold about twelve minutes. He parked the truck on the main road and looked around to make sure he was not seen by anyone before he proceeded to Mary Logan's house. He went around the house to a window; it was her room. He had been there more than a couple of times, watching Mary Logan, getting himself acquainted with everything about the house and her routine.

She worked in a small ice cream shop off Chillicothe Road, and if she was not at work then she would be at home, no friends, no family. Harold had previously wondered why Mary Logan kept away from the rest of her friends. He had concluded that since they were now well-known figures in Kirtland, they had simply refused to associate with a junkie. But after the events of the party, he understood the drama that had gone down among the group.

Since he had been watching her, Harold realized what an easy target Mary Logan was. The fact that the old house was the only one around the area contributed a lot to that. He noticed that she did not have much to do, apart from tending to a flower garden she kept behind the house. Mary Logan would rather live in seclusion, away from the people of Kirtland, who all had one thing or the other to say about her life.

A dim light shone in Mary's room. Harold saw that she was asleep. He went to the rear door and pointed his tiny torchlight toward it. He brought out another knife, an army knife with several blades. He pushed one of them through the knob, twisted it sideways, and the door immediately made a sound. It was opened.

The door led to the kitchen. Harold saw that she kept a tidy kitchen. He advanced quietly to her room to find the bed empty. *She must have heard some sound,* he thought instantly. Suddenly, he heard a loud shriek behind him and before he could turn to see what was going on, a numbing pain landed on his back. He staggered forward and held the bed frame for support. He turned quickly to see Mary Logan with a baseball bat. With a jerking motion, she threw the bat at him and ran out of the room.

Harold swerved away from it and dashed after her, ignoring the thumping pain. He caught up with her in the living room and dragged her by the arm. Mary tried to wriggle free but Harold was too strong for her, yet she did not give up. She tried continuously to twist her way out of his hands.

Mary knew that shouting for help was pointless and she had a feeling that her attacker was aware too. She charged at him with her other hand but he caught her. Harold pulled her closer and pressed her body tightly to him with one hand.

"Who are you?" she yelled. "Why do you wanna kill me?" If this was the same person that killed Alice and Brenda, Mary did not understand why he was trying to kill her too.

Before she could utter another word, Harold stabbed her with his father's pocket knife. It went through her side and she lost every ounce of strength she had left. Mary fell on the floor as Harold released his grip on her. Mary's breathing slowed. She let out a low whimper. Her eyes were closing up. She tried to keep them open but they would not stay open. She was losing blood too quickly. She made an effort to get a clear view of her attacker's face but the light was too dim to make out any distinctive features.

He stared down at her. His anger built up rapidly as old memories flushed through him. He bent down and continued to put the knife through her haphazardly, grunting with each stab. After a while, he stopped, panting loudly. He stood on his feet and got a proper look at the person before him. It looked nothing like the woman he had been struggling with earlier.

A new wave of rage flowed deep into his head. He was angry at the dead Mary Logan for making him make a mess out of her death. If only she had stayed asleep rather than making futile attempts to defend herself. Though he prepared for it, he preferred to kill his victims at the site where their body would be found and not in their home. He was only meant to kill them in their home when it was the last thing left to do. But Mary Logan's effort to defend herself had made him lose his temper.

Harold went into her room. He needed to find something to wrap her dead body since he couldn't have her blood dripping all the way as he carried her to the truck.

He ruffled through Mary Logan's things, he was becoming impatient. He had been there way too long. The room had a tiny closet. It looked scanty and unused. He pointed his torchlight around until it stopped on a material that seemed like polyester. It was a raincoat. Red. Harold took it and went back to the living room. He wrapped her body with the raincoat. It was big enough, probably for someone as huge as himself.

He left the house. He dropped the body in the back seat. Harold checked his watch, it read thirteen minutes to eleven. He drove off silently from the neighborhood and headed to the east branch of the Chagrin. It was going to be an eleven-minute drive.

Chapter 7

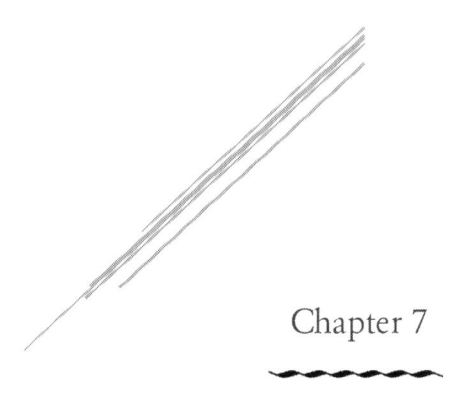

The Kirtland Killer

Detective Stapleton was not sure about what he was hoping to find this early in the forest where Brenda Johnson's body was found. He still believed that he was not alone that day in the Gildersleeve Mountains, that someone was watching him. So, if there was a chance that it was the killer, he had hoped to meet him here one day.

He knew what his partner would say if he told him that he came there every day hoping to catch the killer revisiting the scene. Smith would laugh and tell him that the killer would not be that foolish, and that was why he did not tell him. Stapleton had thought about it several times and it did not seem likely to him either, but he could not shake off the urge to come here every morning.

He saw a bough not too far away. He moved closer and was about to sit when he heard something ruffling through the woods. He immediately removed his gun from the holster. He pointed it forward and scanned around, then the sound came again. It was a squirrel. *I'm in a forest. What do I expect?* he thought. He left the woods and went into the car.

Chief Horning spoke to him the previous day. He said the mayor was becoming impatient. People were starting to make conclusions that the Kirtland killer was smarter than the police and he would not be found. Many from Tony Adolf's camp used the bad press to their advantage. So, the mayor's attitude was understandable. Stapleton turned the ignition and drove away.

He met Smith at the precinct. He was going through the documents they got from Kirtland High School.

"Morning, man," Smith said as he saw him, his expression showing that he had been waiting for Stapleton. "You heard what the news is saying?"

"What?"

"They've given the killer a name, the Kirtland Killer. And people are saying he's smarter than the police."

"Yeah, I heard about that. Works from Tony Adolf."

"Is this a joke to him? Two people are dead for God's sake."

"He is a politician, Jake."

"I can't believe this is happening." Smith looked confused.

"So, how's Maureen?" Stapleton asked him. He had been thinking about them for a while but he wanted to give it time. It felt like the right time now.

Smith looked away from his partner and if Stapleton did not know better, he would have thought that he did not hear his question.

"She said she's leaving," he finally replied. "I talked to her like you said and she told me she can't continue the marriage anymore. She said it's boring." His voice faded as he said the last sentence.

"What about the kids?"

"I don't know what she wants to do with them. She's not talking to me."

Stapleton moved closer to his partner and patted him on the shoulder. He remembered when he saw that the couple was having some issues with their marriage. It was Smith's birthday and he had invited him over for dinner at their house, a move that was more because he needed someone to bail him out when it starts getting awkward between them than wanting his partner to celebrate his birthday with him.

They had gone to their house together from work that day, and from the first moment he spent seeing the couple together, he had felt the coldness between them. Over dinner, he saw how they reacted when their hands collided when they both reached for the salt after he had asked for it. Even the way they both insisted on putting the kids to bed was a world war of words, in their case the words were sedulously short and well chosen.

Stapleton had never been in a marriage of his own, but in the few relationships he had been in the past, he knew how tough they had been for him.

***

Sunny took a last look at herself in the mirror. She faked a smile as she patted down her long hair. The red, fitting dress she had on hugged her shape elegantly. It had a gold belt round it, at the waist. No matter what was happening in her life, she had to look happy. Since her parents died and she started living with her uncle's family, she had grown up to be his right hand, and consequently, she had been thrown under the same limelight as him. It became even more intense when her uncle became the mayor. She began to show interest in his affairs when she noticed that even though her uncle would love his own daughter to be involved in his political career, she was not in the least interested. Even his wife did everything she did out of obligation.

What better way to show gratitude to him for taking me in and caring for me like his own daughter? Sunny thought. To her surprise, Paul wasted no time in entrusting her with his works. She helped him with several of his documents and sometimes they spent time together talking about his plans. She saw that it made him happy and Sunny gradually grew into working with him. After she left college, Paul charged her with even more responsibilities. And by the time Paul was elected as mayor, Sunny was already known throughout Kirtland as Paul Griffith's diligent right hand. The media credited her industriousness as the main reason for her uncle's success.

If she was to be honest, she enjoyed it all. She took delight in the admiration she got from the public. Whenever her uncle called her out in a public function, she liked the way people applauded her. But at the moment, she wished she were just an ordinary person, free from all the public attention. After everything that she had learned from that night at the party, her whole life felt like a lie. It seemed to her like she had been living a life that was not in any way her own. The man she loved the most turned out to have been lying to her all this while. Even the friends she thought she knew kept her in the dark about things that closely concerned her. She could not help but doubt everything she had with them over the past decade.

Mary must have felt betrayed after what we did to her, she realized. Everything made sense to Sunny now, the sudden change in Mary's attitude toward her. It must have been really tough for her, seeing Sunny like that, knowing that she was the reason for her rejection among her friends. After everything that Mary had gone through, she did not deserve such treatment. No one deserved that. She was sure it would not be enough but she needed to apologize to Mary for everything she went through because of her.

She had thought about what she would say to her and what Mary's reaction would be, and that had been Sunny's excuse for pushing her visit to Mary's place for the past few days. However, she was ready to see her now and do what had been meant to be done all these years. Sunny finally left her house for Maple Street.

At Mary's house, after she got no response from knocking at her front door, it occurred to Sunny that she had not considered the fact that Mary might not be at her house. She had expected to find her at home. She looked around the area. There was no house or neighbor to ask anything from. She remembered instantly that she worked in an ice cream shop. She knew where it was but it was inappropriate to visit her at her workplace to discuss personal matters.

The whole area looked abandoned, she observed. Sunny wondered how Mary was able to live there alone. Then she thought, if there was anyone she knew that was capable of living in such a place alone like this, it was Mary Logan. She had always been the tough one. Together with Alice, she had known her since elementary school.

Mary had no issues going physically against boys back then. She remembered a day in middle school when she attacked a group of boys that were taunting a wounded rabbit. The boys had been so scared by the toothless girl from nowhere that charged violently at them. She chased them off the rabbit and carried it to the school's agriculture teacher. Sunny had been really impressed by her actions and she wished she could stand up against boys for good causes like that.

Sunny decided to leave. She would have to check on her some other time. Somehow, she felt relieved that at least she did not have to face Mary that afternoon. As soon as she turned to leave, her eyes drew to what looked like drops of a dark red, almost brown, substance. Sunny moved closer, and immediately she saw that it was blood. Something rose in her chest. She was enclosed in a cloud of fear at the thoughts that went through her head. Had Mary been attacked too? She quickly went back to the door and knocked louder than she had done earlier.

In a frantic motion, she went round the house and saw that the rear door was left ajar. She rushed into the house. In the living room, Sunny met the carpet splattered with blood, it was thick and horrifying. She covered her mouth as she moved closer. They had gotten to Mary too. She could feel her limbs weakening. It was as if a sacrifice had been made in Mary's living room.

It was now evident that someone was targeting them and Sunny understood she was in danger of becoming the next victim. She ran out of the house as she began to feel like she wanted to throw up. She had never seen so much human blood in her life. She knew she had to notify the detectives as soon as possible, so she went straight to the Kirtland Police Department.

When Sunny stormed into the KPD building, a lot of eyes stared at her with surprise. They wondered what the mayor's famous niece was doing in the police station, sweating so much and looking like she was being chased. Sunny was not bothered by the attention, rather she went straight to a uniformed man and asked for Detective Stapleton. Hearing the urgency in her words and seeing the look on her face, the officer asked no question as he led her to the office where she met the two detectives, eating lunch. Smith was finishing the last portion of a bowl of chili, while Stapleton had a half-eaten glazed ham sandwich on a plate before him. Sunny ran in after the officer.

"Ms. Griffith, what a surprise!" Smith said, after which he immediately pushed a small bottle of water down his throat.

"They've gotten to Mary too," Sunny said. The only thing the two men could hear was the fear in her voice. "You've got to do something, anything!"

Stapleton moved a chair closer to Sunny and directed her to sit. Then he said to her, "Tell us what happened exactly, Ms. Griffith."

"There was blood everywhere, so much blood." Sunny's face had gone pale. She looked as if she had just seen a ghost. Thinking about what she saw made her more scared than when she saw it.

"Ms. Griffith, take a deep breath and tell us exactly what happened and we'll take it from there," Stapleton said to her.

Sunny took a moment to gather herself together, then she started, "I went to her house," she gave a gulp before she continued, "I went to Mary's house. I wanted to apologize for everything we've done to her. I knocked but I got no answer. Then I remembered she worked in an ice cream shop not far from here and when I was about to leave, I saw blood on the ground. So, I decided to check the rear door and it was opened. No one was in the house. All I found was blood splattered all over her living room." Sunny broke into tears.

"Did you find Mary anywhere in the house?"

"No. Just blood all over the place."

The detectives looked at each other. The killer had struck again, and if they could find Mary Logan's body just like the rest, then it would be firmly established that he was out to kill the five ladies. It pained Stapleton to realize that he had just succeeded in killing three of them and there was nothing he could do to stop him from doing that.

The men prepared for Mary Logan's house. They told Sunny that it was best she left her apartment and stayed at the mayor's house— which was more secured— for a while. And if she was able to get across to Elise McKennie, she had to inform her too.

"It's all my fault. I kept pushing back my visit. I should have gone there earlier. Now it's too late and I'm probably not gonna get a chance to talk to her ever again," Sunny said in between sobs, ignoring what the detectives had just told her.

"Ms. Griffith, this is definitely not your fault. But you have to do what we told you. Stay at the mayor's house for now," Smith instructed her in a firm tone.

"Okay, I'll do that." Sunny replied.

The two men left the precinct.

When the detectives entered Mary Logan's living room and they saw the horrendous mess the killer made, it became clear to them what kind of killer they were looking for. It was one that bore a deep grudge against these ladies.

"What kind of psychopath would do this?" Smith said, exclaiming in dismay at the sight.

"Mary must have put up a serious fight," Stapleton said, as the men examined other parts of the house. They saw that a few things were out of place, including the baseball bat. "He must be getting impatient."

"What do you mean?" Smith asked his partner.

"With the way he killed the previous victims, it was clear that he did not want any bloodshed."

"Maybe Mary really did put up a good fight."

"It doesn't matter that she did. There was evidence that suggested that Alice Panabaker did so too, but he was patient enough to handle her without having to shed blood. He was carving out a style. He must be getting really impatient to ditch it, and that's how we are gonna catch him because he'll definitely make a mistake and when he does, we have to capitalize on that." Stapleton sounded sure of what he was saying. Smith had never heard him say so many words at once.

"Well, we still need to find the body to confirm anything," Smith noted to his partner.

"We'll find the body because he certainly wants us to. It's his game but not for very long. He's gonna lose control of it very soon," Stapleton replied. "Radio for the forensics team. We need to have this place scrubbed. If there was anything he left behind, even a strand of his hair, I want it found."

"Sure."

"We need to inform Chief Horning. He's got to put together that search party one more time. Hopefully for the last time. Mary Logan's body is probably lying somewhere with her head under water."

A few minutes later, KPD cars flooded the area. The sirens replaced the hollow silence and when they walked out to meet them. They saw that Chief Horning came with the lads too. The old man carried a disturbed look on him as they saw him getting out of his wagon. His shoulders appeared sagged from carrying the chaos that came with the killings.

"I came as soon as I heard. What do we have?"

"The body is missing but the place is a shithell. With all due respect, you should brace yourself, Chief," Smith informed him.

"We need to begin the search as soon as possible. The earlier we find the body, the better," Stapleton wasted no time. "There would definitely be something on this one. He was rough, he must have slipped somewhere."

"Bowman and his men are already on their way. They've gathered the town boys. We'll join them from here." Chief matched the urgency in his tone. He wanted the killings to come to a full stop sooner than anyone there. "But are we sure it's the same killer?"

A new kind of enthusiasm filled Stapleton's tone. "We've previously speculated a connection that this murder, if confirmed, would firmly establish. My professional guess is that it is the same killer."

When Chief Horning saw Mary's living room, he was thankful Smith had warned him earlier. He wondered what the body would look like if the scene looked like this. What kind of heartless person would do this to a person? He must have drained every ounce of blood from the victim. There were blood splashes all over the wall. It was an abomination.

The men stepped aside and allowed forensics to do their job. The white-suited men went through everything piece by piece, scrubbing, gathering and bagging what they could. Smith and Stapleton offered to join Chief Horning's search party and the men left the place.

Chapter 8

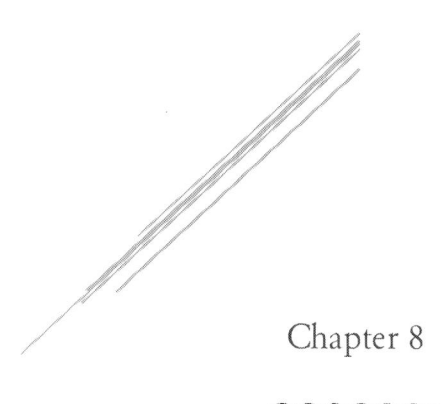

Another Murder

"I can think of a million ways I'd rather be spending my evening than scouring through bushes." Blair slapped his left forearm as he protested for the thousandth time. "These mosquitoes aren't making it easier."

"I have one particular thing in mind," Kelly, his partner in crime, replied. His eyes sparkled as he gave Blair a knowing look.

"What else could it be other than that girl you just met?"

"You know right."

"Remind me again why I'm subjecting myself to insect bites because of rich people's kids." Blair's irritation had gotten to its peak and his friend knew it.

"I heard the one we're looking for isn't rich at all. Heard it was a blood fest in her living room."

"I don't get it. Why would you kill her in her living room and move the body elsewhere so we can find it?"

"Dude is crazy. He's showing off or something."

Kelly had a young neighbor, a policeman, and he was his go-to for updates concerning the Kirtland Killer cases. He was the one that pushed him to volunteer for the search party if he wanted to get firsthand information since he seemed interested. The truth was, everyone in Kirtland was interested, even people like Blair that fronted with indifference. In his own case, his father was a policeman. He had been forced to volunteer against his will.

They approached a steep area near the Chagrin River, east branch. The two young men jogged down the steep decline, the rest of the crew, including Officer Bowman, close behind them. It was getting darker. The barks from the police dogs were becoming annoying for Blair.

"If they have the dogs, why do they need us?" He hit his right foot against a stone and cursed out loudly.

"I'm sorry, Blair. I'm the one with the torch."

"It's okay. I'll live." He was done checking out the foot. "Now, let's see if our body is in that water."

Kelly was surprised. He had just hit his foot against a stone, he did not understand his sudden interest in finding the body. "Thought you didn't care about the body," he said.

"I don't. But since my dad has forced me here, I might as well be the one to find the body. Maybe he'd let me use his bike for once."

Kelly grinned at his friend's words; he knew he had always been interested. That was why anytime they met, he asked questions that would instigate him to recount all the recent news he had heard from his neighbor. If he was so interested, he could have asked his dad. Kelly was sure he would be more than happy to share some. He pointed the torchlight to the water, scanning from left to right. It was a flowing river, not wide at all.

Blair spotted it. "Stop! I saw something." He snatched the torch from him and ran forward. He pointed the torch to Mary's legs first, all the way up to her immersed head. It was all covered in blood, as if she'd been bathed in her own blood.

"Holy shit!" Kelly had anticipated finding the body all day but seeing it now, he was nauseated. He turned his back on it and threw up by the river side.

Blair called out to the rest, "I found something! I've found the body!"

Sounds from several feet hitting the ground repeatedly filled the area. Someone blew a whistle and the crew from the other side could be heard running toward them too. Blair searched for his father's face and when he saw him, he cherished the proud look on his face. He had been waiting for this moment for a long time.

Officer Bowman radioed the chief's crew, they had gone elsewhere. He thanked the men and pleaded with them to step backward, and head home. He explained that it was a crime scene now and they would need to keep the place as it is, until the forensics team and the appropriate guys have had a chance to examine it properly.

The men slowly retreated with grumbles and hisses. They felt they had been used and when it got to the real excitement, they sent them back home. Bowman shook Blair's hand and dismissed him. Blair grabbed Kelly, who was still recovering from the shock, and they left with the other men.

By the time the chief got there with the detectives, the area was totally free of volunteers. Everyone around was uniformed. The forensics team were already on site and they had begun their work.

"What on earth!" Smith exclaimed as they pulled Mary's bloody head from the water.

Chief Horning could only express his sadness in silence. He was too tired to use any other method. His aging limbs were burning out and at that moment, all he wanted to do was get on a bed.

Stapleton, on the other hand, just got the confirmation he was waiting for. Without any doubt, this killer had a connection to Kirtland High School and he was going to find it. He was not going to rest if he did not. Now, if he could just find the truck Tyron Baker had claimed to see.

He turned to Smith and said to him, "Our work just got messier."

Smith looked at Mary Logan's body as it was being bagged and the words of his partner appeared vividly before him.

***

Thirty-five stab wounds. Smith repeated in his head after Dr. Peralta. No wonder there was so much blood. What could these ladies have done to offend the killer? What could Mary Logan have done to deserve this? He could not come up with anything. Dr. Peralta's sing-song voice geared him out of his head.

"It's everywhere, to the chest, abdomen, head, thighs, one to the right eye, everywhere. She certainly would have been dead after the first three stabs and felt nothing afterwards. Around thirty of them appeared to have been delivered post-mortem," Dr. Peralta continued.

Smith was a little bit relieved by that piece of information. He could not imagine someone having to go through that horror.

"One of the first few hits must have been delivered right here," he pointed to the upper right portion of the body's abdomen. "That explains why there was so much blood." The expression on Dr. Peralta's face was one of a math teacher who just made calculus easy for his students. His tiny frame shifted easily about the lab as he explained and revealed details to the men— which included Chief Horning, the two detectives and Officer Bowman.

He was a highly intelligent man. Stapleton once acknowledged to his partner that he was the most brilliant M.E. he had ever seen in his career. Chief Horning considered him a great asset in the KPD and he never hesitated to say that to him at every chance he got. But to Dr. Peralta himself, it was all child's play.

He was fascinated by crime and mysteries since he was young and after he graduated from medical school, he knew this was what he would do, much to the amazement of his friends that thought he would follow a more lucrative path. Considering how exceptional he was in medical school, he was tipped to go right to the top but what they did not know was that he had chosen his own path even before medical school.

"Now to the interesting part," Dr. Peralta got into one of his animated gestures. "The deepest wound, which I presume to be the first, went through her right side."

Stapleton wanted to ask him why he thought it was the first stab but he remembered Dr. Peralta's remark about asking questions while he was revealing his findings. Specifically, he emphasized that he most likely was going to answer any question they have as he went on, and if he did not, the question could be asked after he was done and not before. He was that kind of man. Systematic to a fault.

On most occasions though, he provided answers to their questions before he was done and he would add things like to answer any question you might have been courting after he had in fact answered one of the men's questions along the way. He was well respected for this.

"I was able to extract a wood fragment from the wound. After I had carefully examined it and put it through some process of science, I was able to reach the conclusion that it was from the knife. It must have fallen off the handle as he pushed the knife in. Then it occurred to me, where else would it be from? I know I don't have a piece of wood embedded in me!" He was the only one that laughed at his joke, a tiny toned, short-lived laugh.

"It could be from the woods," Stapleton said, to direct his attention back to the topic. He knew that before he could conclude it was from the knife, he had made certain of it and he had an explanation, which as it turned out, he did.

"Of course, that's a possibility." He pointed his left index finger to Stapleton. "You've always been one of the brightest, Detective Stapleton, and that's what I like about you."

Bowman let out a silent laugh. Dr. Peralta's personality was why he was there. He had no real business being there at all but he loved to see him go about his business and how he could make just about anyone look like a kid, even big men like Stapleton. And that was in contrast to his height.

"Except that a piece of wood off a hardwood tree would not look so carefully carved as this." He lifted the wood fragment from a stainless plate on his table, just beside the corpse. None of the men had noticed it. He passed it to Stapleton. "Don't worry, it's sterile. I made my findings, and the fragment was regular with the pattern of knife handles that was made in the seventeenth century, precisely for pocket knives. Now, what we are talking about here is an expensive piece of cutlery, even back then. My guess is it's from Rome, but that's beside the point. The point, gentlemen, is that your killer is a rich personality who is able to purchase such a high value antique or it was something he inherited. Or he could have simply stolen it," he shrugged off the last sentence.

He added, raising his left index once again, "The fragment covered the edge of the handle and that made it easy for me if you're wondering." They were not. At least not about how he was able to trace the fragment to knife handles that was made back in the seventeenth century.

He was the wonder. He had almost single-handedly given them their first real lead. They were all more than impressed. Stapleton had discarded the question he wanted to ask, even though he did not provide an answer to that particular question, the good doctor had given him an answer to the big question that hung over them. Who was the killer?

The wood fragment was with Chief Horning now. He held the material close to his eyes as though if he looked closely, he would see why Dr. Peralta said it was that expensive. Dr. Peralta's sudden interjection drew his attention back.

"Yes! The last observation I made was that judging by the reputation of these kinds of knives I'm talking about, it wasn't meant to break off easily. Maybe," he raised his favorite finger, "mind you, this is just a narrow assumption, a number of factors might have been in play. Maybe, the knife was not stored properly and it became out of shape for a while before it found usage again."

"That would make the assumption that it was stolen more probable," Smith pointed out.

"I'll leave that to you, after all, you guys are the detectives," Dr. Peralta replied and laughed out loud in his melodious manner.

Putting the pieces together, they were looking for a large male, coordinated, probably rich and has a connection to Kirtland High School. Stapleton felt optimistic for the first time about this case. It had taken Mary Logan to lose her life too before they could get something off him. He knew he was going to make a mistake, call it impatience, call it arrogance. It was bound to happen at a point. It was painful that three people were already dead. He had just spoken with Mary Logan not long ago. He sat across her in the same room she was murdered. This one was not going to escape his memories and when he finally found the killer. He would make sure he paid for what he had done to these ladies.

The next morning, the detectives were at Tony Adolf's house, seated on a grey two-seater in the outermost room of the house. They had been told by a man that Elise Mckennie, together with Tony Adolf was in an important meeting and they could either come back or wait for the meeting to end.

The man had been polite. He was tall and lean. He appeared to have been one of the several people that worked for Tony Adolf. The detectives knew he was rich, but not this rich. His house was a mansion. It was situated a few miles into Kirtland from the south. It was a twenty-minute drive from the Kirtland Police Department.

Stapleton examined the interior of the room, everything looked regal. It made him wonder how the interior of the living area of the house looked. The wall clock was silver-plated, it was what stood out to Stapleton. It was large and hung against the wall opposite him. It shined brightly from the white light that the chandelier produced. Lion heads were engraved on the edges. The heads pushed out a little, giving the wall clock a special look.

THE KIRTLAND KILLER

Smith finally spoke out what they had both been thinking, "I didn't know Tony Adolf was wealthy like this." He turned to Stapleton, bearing his amusement all on his face.

"Me either, I guess you would have to know him personally to really know."

The man came back again. "Gentlemen, they are now waiting for you in the living room. Please follow me."

They went after him, into a larger room, where Elise Mckennie sat beside her cousin, smiling from ear to ear.

"Good morning, detectives," she called as soon as she saw them. "Nice to see you once again. Gladly, under better circumstances."

They shook hands with Tony Adolf.

"I doubt that." Smith wiped the smile off her face. "This is not a social call. You might not have heard, but Mary Logan is dead. Her body was recently found. I'll spare you the details but what's important is that you have to be careful from now on. It is clear that someone is targeting you and your friends. He has succeeded in killing three and there are only two left, which includes you. You might be the next target."

Elise went white by Smith's revelation. The whole thing just got scary. Was someone really out to kill her and her friends? Why? She became confused and did not know what to think. She looked intermittently from the detectives to her cousin. Finally, she was able to mutter a question.

"So, Mary is really dead?"

"She is." It was Stapleton that confirmed her friend's death to her. "And we want you to take precautions now." Turning to Tony Adolf through the last sentence.

Tony Adolf got the cue. "Of course. We have a security team on the premises and Elise stays here with us for now."

"Nice. Ms. Mckennie, it is advised you continue to stay here while we try to find the person doing this."

All she could do was nod in response. The news of Mary's death and hearing that someone was after her life had left her in shock. She had thought that, after Alice and Brenda's death, it was too forward to conclude that they were being targeted. She told Sunny the same thing when she suggested it to her. Words of her cousin Sunny came to her mind. They were both the last ones alive now. She had been right all along. She asked the detectives, "How's Sunny doing?"

"She is finding it hard to wrap her head around it all. She was the one that discovered that Mary had been attacked when she went to her house so she's a little bit shaken up," Smith explained.

All she could do was shake her head in disbelief. She looked lost in thought then she turned to Stapleton suddenly, "why do you think we are being targeted, Detective?"

"We've not made a direct connection for now, but we are edging closer and we believe that it has to do with your time together at Kirtland High School. If there's anything that you can tell us, please do so."

Kirtland High? Elise thought it was unbelievable, why would their time in high school be the reason they were being murdered one by one? She tried thinking of something, anything. Blank. For God's sake, they were just teenagers like everyone else. Maybe the detectives were wrong. But she gave it a second thought. What other reason could there be? Alice had left Kirtland almost immediately after high school, and they had alienated Mary around the same.

She felt guilty thinking about how they had treated Mary. She wished she had done better. Now she's dead and she never got a chance to apologize. She bit her lip. If the detectives were right then it was beyond her why they murdered her friends because of their high school days.

Tony Adolf thanked the men as they took their leave. He promised to provide to them all the resources they needed to catch the killer that posed a threat to his cousin's life. They should not hesitate to ask him anything. He could not resist the opportunity, so he added, "I know our policemen are working hard and trying their best. What they need is proper management and my administration promises to give that to them."

Smith, who had noted how he stood clear of their entire discussion, had given him credit for understanding boundaries. Now all that is in the trash. The man was just like he had heard. It appeared he was just waiting for the right opportunity to pounce on. What a shame!

***

Harold had been watching Sunny all through the class. He had not picked up anything the teacher had been saying. It was history. He cared less about it. His

THE KIRTLAND KILLER

own was disgusting enough. He would rather wish to forget it as quickly as possible. The teacher's voice and the rest of the activities that went on all formed background noise. What mattered to Harold was the beautiful girl with the longest hair, who sat two chairs forward to his right. She was his focus. He let his mind explore different possibilities with Sunny as the center of attention.

Immediately the bell rang and everyone started moving out of the class. He noticed Sunny was particularly in a hurry to make her way out, which explained why she kept looking at the wall clock during the class. Harold had thought they had cheerleading practice but Alice did not look in a hurry. In fact, she sat back, talking to another girl from the class.

In the hallway, Sunny walked even faster. Harold could not keep up. He continued to locate and lose her in the crowd of students that flooded the hallway. She was really far in front and hurrying along. Harold's height was the only reason he could see her at all. When his eyes picked her up again, she was removing a book from her locker. She placed the book in her bag and continued toward the exit. Harold increased his steps and followed her out of Kirtland High School.

Outside, she had turned and continued down the left side of the road. Harold was surprised, he had never seen Sunny storm out of school so early after official school hours. If there was no cheerleading practice, then she would be hanging out with her friends, talking and giggling or they would watch the football team do their practice if there was one. It appeared that they trained every time. He was curious about what Sunny had to do that she left the school surroundings so early, earlier than she normally did. So, he followed her.

Not that he had anything to do with his afternoon other than going home to his wasted mother who had been drinking a lot more than she normally did lately. The result showed in her rants, they had increased too. She would go on and on about different topics, some included Harold and most didn't.

Among those that had to do with him was the one about him being the reason she became like this. She would have become a successful lawyer, the most successful one in the whole of Kirtland if he had not come unexpectedly. Another one was that Harold stuck out like a sore thumb, just like his father and that they were both the reason for her misfortune. Considering how much his father left behind for her and her lavish lifestyle, Harold thought she was her own misfortune.

The other rants that had nothing to do with Harold touched some rather more subtle topics. She mentioned names he did not know and had never heard before and talked about members of a circle he thought did not probably exist. Harold quietly concluded that she was crazy and that it was better he stayed off her path. So, any opportunity to delay his arrival was welcomed.

He continued slowly after her. He knew Sunny must not see him following her so he kept a bit far behind. She stopped at a place and bought snacks, pie, and ice cream. She continued on her way and ate while walking. After she was done eating, she resumed her previous manner of walking— quick and purposeful. Harold was still trying to figure out where she was headed. Not home definitely, she would have turned right from school.

She took another turn into another street. It looked like a factory area. Harold hid behind a van and waited for her to complete her turn. After a while, he pushed forward and continued after her. She was gone. An open place with big, heavy looking abandoned factory machines was all he could see. Then he listened carefully after some sounds. It was the sound of people talking. But from where? It sounded like it was coming from afar, no, like it was coming from the ground.

He almost concluded he was foolish to have thought that the sound was coming from the ground but then he saw the make-shift stairs near the wall. It looked like a ladder but it had some kind of ring around it. The stairs ran down an opening and he realized that the voices were indeed from the ground. There was an underground version of the place where he was standing. He knew if he tried going down there, they would hear him as he approached. And he still did not know the people down there, or if Sunny was even there at all. She seemed to have disappeared in a flash.

He got a better standing position and he was able to see the place really well. He saw different men moving the same thing from one position to another, it was a white rectangular plastic bag. Or the bag was transparent, and it held a white substance, Harold was not sure. He saw Sunny walking past his line of sight with a man who looked like her uncle. It was her uncle. Sunny held a book and wrote in it as they talked.

Harold was confused. Whatever the men were moving in there, he was sure it was not legal. Why else would they be working in an underground abandoned place? Was Sunny involved in one of her uncle's illegal businesses? He had never really trusted her uncle but he thought Sunny would never do anything illegal if she was asked. Harold left that place thinking about what he just saw. He was more than confused. It changed the way he saw Sunny Griffith.

Chapter 9

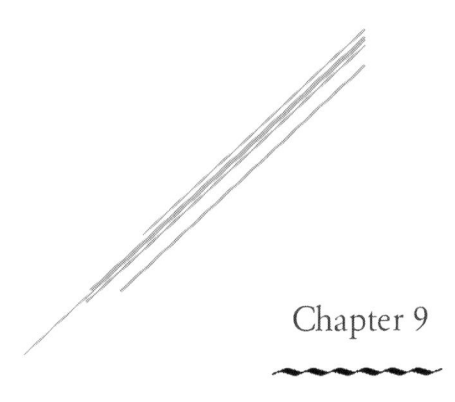

The First Clue

It's been four days since Mary Logan was killed. Detectives Stapleton and Smith had gone to every antique shop in and near Kirtland, none had been productive. They got the same answer. No one has seen a knife with that kind of handle before. At least, they now know Dr. Peralta was right, it was an expensive knife. An old man who owned an antique shop just outside Kirtland confirmed that to them. He said if he had one of those knives, he would sell it for nothing less than a thousand. He had seen it last when he was a very small kid. He told them they were rare to come by.

Stapleton was now leaning more toward the wealthy killer rather than the killer who was also a part-time thief because as it seemed, there was nowhere he could steal it from. And since Dr. Peralta pointed out that it could have been inherited, the wealthy killer was looking more likely. They were edging closer. Stapleton knew that but something was still missing. A last piece of the puzzle that would put an end to everything. It was close but they had not laid their hands on it.

He was back where they found Mary Logan's body. It had become more of a ritual than trying to catch the killer when he came back to the crime scene. It helped him to think and evaluate things. When he was leaving his house this morning and Smith asked him where he was going, he was thankful that he understood when he told him he was coming there. He respected his stance on the matter and did not ask any questions.

Smith had been staying with him since he moved out of the house instead of his wife. Maureen had made it clear that she could not live with him anymore. She wanted to leave the house, without the children. Smith had thought it was only appropriate that he was the one to leave. He couldn't take care of the kids, not with this kind of job.

In the past few days since he had moved in, Stapleton noticed him whenever he slipped into a sad mood, which was the same time every day— during dinner. He must be thinking about the time when his family ate happily together at their table. Stapleton assumed it felt like years ago now. Smith was deeply affected by what his marriage was going through but he tried so much not to show it. His marriage was crumbling right before his own eyes and there was nothing he could do about it.

At least, now they could work the case together anytime, Stapleton concluded. They would have more time together and anything that came to either of their minds could be communicated as soon as possible. He hoped that Smith and his wife would later see beyond whatever was happening between them and move forward.

They had no luck with the truck either. No one had seen any truck that matched the description that Tyron Baker gave them. They went to every public, crowded place in Kirtland but the answer was the same.

Stapleton was done walking around the crime scene. It was a Sunday, so he did not have to go to work. He made his way out of the woods. He was about to enter his car when he saw a familiar figure coming toward him.

He wore a black plain t-shirt that hugged his body, showing his build features. He looked sporty. Stapleton closed the door of his car and met with him on his way.

He held his hand to forehead to remember his name, "Don't say it, I'll remember," it took him a few more seconds, "Harold! Harold Franczyk, right?"

"Yes sir, you are right," he smiled nervously, just the same way he did that night at the mayor's party.

He must really be a shy, mommy's boy. Even with all the muscles.

"What are you doing here?"

"I sometimes jog through the area. It's part of my exercise routine," he said slowly.

Stapleton could never cease to be amazed by how such a huge man could sound so much like a little child. It was fascinating. "Keeping fit as usual. Sorry our meeting was cut short at the party. I hope you enjoyed the rest of it," he teased him. He knew he enjoyed nothing that night. He looked completely out of place. If he had given it another second thought, Harold would have stayed at home.

It was rare for Stapleton to become fond of someone

so quickly, he had only met him for a few minutes at the party but as it was, he liked him.

"What are you doing on Friday? Let's have lunch together. I know a nice spot. Get to know each other and all."

"Uh, Friday doesn't work for me. I have an engagement already. Maybe another time."

Stapleton saw that he had issues with eye contact. He was not used to looking into someone's eyes and telling them your mind. He must have been called a weirdo in high school. He kind of pitied him. He reminded him of his brother.

"No problem then. Would be looking forward to it." He went into his car, brought out a paper and gave it to him. It contained the number he was to ring when he had the time to hangout.

They shook hands and they went their separate ways. Stapleton drove off.

***

Sunny walked past the lawn. She was tired from the day's work. She had left work earlier than usual. Her back ached and what she needed was a hot shower, a delicious meal and a long, quiet sleep. In that order. The gardener that tended to the lawn smiled as he greeted her. They were always happy to see her, because unlike other people that lived in the mayor's house, she was kind to them. She treated them like humans and she knew all of the workers' names. She knew the names of their kids even— if they had any.

The chef was her closest friend, she had two lovely kids. Twin girls. Sunny adored them. Anytime the woman saw Sunny embracing the girls with so much care, it melted her heart. She appreciated it more than when she gave them gifts, which she often did. Sunny went straight into the kitchen to tell her she was famished. The plump woman, who looked even rounder with the apron, told her she was ahead of her. All she had to do was shower and come for her food.

It was one of the days Sunny was thankful she lived in a house with cooks. She could not imagine having to cook with how she felt. She climbed up the stairs and headed for her room. She was about to turn into her room when she heard the rumbling voices down the hallway. It was the mayor's study. He had left his office earlier and told her he wanted to attend an important meeting with some associates. He did not sound as if the meeting was going to be at home.

Sunny felt uncomfortable. The way he had fidgeted when he told her was suspicious. *Maybe it's my head that was causing me to think too much,* she thought. She wanted to let it go but then the mayor never attended any meeting with some associates that Sunny did not know about. She walked quietly closer to the room and pinned her ear to the door.

"So, what are you gonna call it?" She was certain that was Paul's voice.

"Call it a heart attack or something. This isn't the first time that Fortune would be doing this, Mayor. Rest assured, it won't blow up on your face. You just do your part." The voice sounded familiar, but Sunny could not place it on anyone yet.

A third voice said, "Now that we've eliminated your threat to re-election, may we discuss the next steps?"

"I still don't feel comfortable saying it like that. A woman was just killed for Christ's sake. I'll discuss it when I'm certain it will be as you assured me. Till then, meeting's over."

Sunny hurried away from the doorway back into her room. What had she just heard? Someone was killed for

Paul's re-election and they were going to call it a heart-attack? Who was Fortune? Who were those men? Could Paul really have supported that they killed someone? It suddenly felt cold in her room. She went to her door and waited until she heard footsteps approaching, then she opened the door to make it look like a coincidence. She had to see the men's faces.

The voice that sounded familiar belonged to Philip Baker, Tyron's father. The other one was a man she did not know but she was sure she had seen him before. Was he Fortune?

Philip was the first to say something, "Hey, the pretty princess. It's been a while. How's it going with managing our dear town?" Apparently, his son took his height from him, he was the type of man that was carelessly too sure about himself. His stride implied it. The smug he carried on his face implied it. The way he patronized people with his words implied it.

Sunny squeezed a smile of some sort. "Good afternoon, Mr. Baker."

"Oh, call me Philip, uh? I'm sure Paul must have taught you to be overly courteous but don't you use that with me," he said. His laughter filled the hallway. He tilted his way backward to the rhythm of the laughter.

Sunny said nothing.

The other man just smiled and waved. Sunny studied his face closely. She did not want to forget it, especially if he was Fortune. The man felt a little bit uneasy by Sunny's cold stare. He quickly looked away and moved forward when he felt that it was becoming awkward.

"I didn't know the important meeting you had was here at home," she said to Paul.

"Yeah, we'll talk about it later," turning to the men, he said, "Gentlemen, let me see you off."

They left.

When Paul came back upstairs, Sunny was waiting for him where he had left her.

"I was not expecting you to be home early." He spoke casually, as if they had not just talked about how they conspired to kill someone because of his re-election. His expression was plain. Sunny looked for a hint of guilt, she did not find one.

"If I had been asked to testify with my life, I would have testified that I knew about every one of your conducts." Sunny was giving him a chance. She wanted to push him, maybe he would talk if she did. She was using the last bit of trust she had in her. "I guess I would have died like a fool as it turned out to be."

"Don't be excessive, Sunny," he was playing it down with a laugh. Just like a guilty person would. "It was just boy's business."

Sunny was angered by those words, boy's business. "Oh, I see, the important meeting with some associates has just turned to boy's business," she tilted her sideways as she said the last two words.

Paul became impatient. "Listen Sunny, I can conduct business with whomever I want to and that's none of your goddamn business!"

Sunny was relieved that his wife and daughter were not around to hear his yell. Then she thought he would not have acted this way if they were. Neither would she. They would have taken it to his study like they normally handled issues. But this was no ordinary issue, someone was killed for Paul's sake and he approved it, if not sanctioned it.

Since he was not going to break, Sunny went straight for it. She had given him enough chances to talk. "Who's Fortune? Who did you kill for your re-election?" Sunny stepped back from him and pointed her finger to him. "I know about everything. I heard you and those bastards talk about it so don't even attempt to lie because if you do, I'll make sure the whole of Kirtland knows about it. Sooner or later, the news of the person you killed will come out and I'll know who it is."

Paul's features softened. His brows depressed and his cheeks narrowed. He opened his mouth to say something but he could not gather his voice. He knew this meant the end to his political career, one he had slowly built over the years. He had not even been to congress yet or assume the office of Ohio State Governor. He had earlier disagreed with the plan but he had been pushed to it, at least that was what he told himself.

He fell on his knees and started begging. "I'm sorry, Sunny. I had no other choice."

Sunny had never seen him like that before. She was embarrassed but that did not conquer the anger in her, if that was what he was trying to do. Sunny demanded him to tell her who they killed. He just kept begging her, his white shirt was dampened by sweat that rose from all the parts of his body, all the way from his head.

"Paul?" His wife and daughter met them there, Sunny and Paul had not heard when they climbed the stairs. They were surprised, expectedly, to see Paul on the floor, begging. His wife was eager to know why her husband was on the floor before Sunny. "What are you doing Paul?" She looked at Sunny and Paul, waiting for an answer from one of them.

Paul could not even look at his own wife. Paul realized that his situation had just got worse. Now, he had to beg the three of them because Sunny would definitely tell.

Sunny told them what had happened and immediately left the scene. She was angry that he had not yet revealed who they killed.

That night, the three other Griffiths came into Sunny's room to plead with her. His wife spoke first. "I'm still finding it difficult to wrap my head around the fact that Paul sanctioned the death of an innocent person. This is certainly not the Paul we know," she said, pointing at her husband.

His daughter said nothing. She must have been forced against her free will. She never really got along with Sunny since they were young. Sunny was just two years older.

Sunny demanded to know who they had killed. "Who was the person they killed?"

"It was Anne Franczyk." Paul said, he could not say anything else. It was his wife that continued the rest.

When the news brought it out that she died of a heart attack the next day, she was meant to stay quiet. Even though she knew it was not true, that it was her uncle, the mayor of the city, that had actually sanctioned her death so that he could get a re-election ticket.

Apparently, the woman was in the circle of a number of Kirtland heavyweights that decided who was to be the next Mayor of Kirtland. Each one of them took a vote before the main elections to determine who they would throw their weight behind as a group. The woman somehow wielded the power of two votes and she was the only one obstructing Paul from getting a re-election ticket, hence her sudden death.

Sunny woke up from her former room in the mayor's house. She did not like the memories that came with the place. After her family had pushed her to choose them over the truth, she had moved out and rented an apartment of her own. Pushed. She realized it was the same words Paul had used back then. They pushed him to accept the offer to kill the woman. Sunny told herself she had no choice, that she could not betray the only family she had left. The same one that had taken her in when she was a child and she had nobody left.

But she had always carried the guilt with her. Now, she was there in the middle of the night, unable to sleep from nightmares of the woman they had killed over a year ago. It felt like she had participated in killing her.

Sunny went back to bed and hoped to sleep. She could only hope since she was going to be there for a while.

***

Crowds, cheers, banners, optimism, water. Lots of water. It was Tony Adolf's campaign day at Kirtland Hills Park. It was buzzing with people. Elise did not expect this kind of turn out, especially with everything that was going on in Kirtland. Tony Adolf was no less surprised. He moved closer to his cousin and informed her about his delight.

"I'm surprised to see so many people," he had the glitters in his eyes. "I'm impressed, thank you, Elise. I owe this to you."

Elise was honored to have been of help. She had to be honest, she had enjoyed every bit of working for this. "Your campaign team did everything, I'm not the only one," she told Tony. He nodded his head in agreement. They were seated under a tent, not far from the main stage. The program had started, and the spokesperson was about to call Tony onto the stage. Elise saw he looked a little bit uptight. He was getting nervous.

She held his hand. "You've got this, Tony. Relax, you've got this."

He nodded his head again as Elise spoke to him. His fiancée was returning from the makeshift mobile toilet that they had provided for people to use in the open space. They hugged each other and she made a gesture and mouthed the words, you got this, baby.

When Tony Adolf climbed the stage and took the microphone, the cheers from the crowd were deafening. Elise could see people screaming for Tony's sake. They lifted their banners and cardboard papers.

"Go Adolf!"

"Kirtland's Golden Boy"

"It starts from within-Adolf"

"Tony Adolf is Mayor"

"The Game Changer"

Elise could see a lot of things written on those papers and she felt emotional thinking about it. When they had started, it had looked as if they would fail. Not that they had won anything yet, but to be able to pull this amount of crowd, she was almost tearful. She looked around to see if no one was looking at her as she dabbed at her eyes with a handkerchief. It was tears of joy. She stood up to ease herself. She had done her part and she was proud of herself.

Harold stood behind the mobile toilet. He had been there for over an hour. He moved slightly away to check out Elise Mckennie for the thousandth time that afternoon. She still was not alone. He knew this was his only chance to get her now. Since he killed Mary Logan, the two remaining girls had been on high alert. Sunny went back to the mayor's house where he wouldn't be able to get his hands on her. It was the same thing as Elise Mckennie. He knew he should not have made such a mess with Mary Logan. He got angry and he lost control.

It was against his plan. He vowed to himself never to lose control like that again. Such display of emotion lead to mistakes and mistakes blow up on one's face. That was it and he knew it. He just was not able to hold himself back that night. Mary Logan had provoked him and it touched his nerve. Now that he was calm and collected, he needed to find a way to get to her.

He was still thinking about alternative plans when he saw Elise Mckennie walking toward the mobile toilet. The gods must be by his side once again. He crouched low and studied her closely. When he was sure that she was really coming to use the toilet, he crouched back to the other side of the mobile toilet. It had four toilets, two for males and two for females. He needed to make sure that whatever Elise Mckennie did, she did not see him coming and he would be able to get to her before she had the chance to shout for help.

It was the perfect time, Tony Adolf had just started speaking. He could hear from the loud speakers and every one there would want to catch the first glimpse of Tony Adolf. So, the chances that they would want to use the toilet are slim. He hoped he was right. He heard the door to one of the toilets open. It was on the male side.

He crouched back to that side. Elise must have missed the male or female sign. He waited for a flushing sound before he approached.

He heard the sound and immediately Elise came out of the toilet. He grabbed her and tightened his hand over her mouth. The gloved hand was so big it covered most of her face. The smell of leather that had been exposed to the sun for a while filled her nose. He wrapped his other arm around her and pulled her to the back of the mobile toilet truck. Her eyes widened as she recognized him. She twisted her body frantically. But she was weak, much weaker than Mary Logan. She stood no chance against Harold. Not the slightest one.

Harold knew he had limited time. He needed to act fast, so he wasted no time. He wrapped his arm around her neck. Before Elise could make use of the opportunity that he had released his hand from her mouth and scream for help, she was already gasping for air. He tightened his grip and held for a minute. He checked for a pulse and found none. He dropped her on the floor and looked around to see if anyone was in the vicinity. He didn't see anyone.

The toilet truck was moved away from the crowd for obvious reasons. He went back behind the truck and carried Elise Mckennie to the female part of the toilets and left the premises.

Tony Adolf had just finished his speech. He almost cried at the end. He glanced to the side and saw his fiancée. Elise's chair was empty. The shouts continued from the crowd.

When he got back to the tent and his fiancée told him that Elise had gone to use the toilet, he was not alarmed at first, but after fifteen minutes, he got up. His action coincided with a sudden rise of noise from the area where the toilet truck was parked. Tony ran down there, his fiancée trailing behind. He slammed his hand against the truck as he saw Elise's body. Her head was in the closet.

That spelled the end of the campaign. Most people flooded back to their home, some stayed though. Detectives Smith and Stapleton were the first to get there. When they got there, they interviewed a few people among the crowd, none of them saw anything. The set of girls that saw the body had only their experience of opening the toilet to find a dead woman to tell.

Soon, Chief Horning, Officer Bowman and the rest got there. They brought Dr. Peralta. Stapleton had requested they bring him along. He could provide them with some useful insights, which he did. He was able to point out a distinct boot print. Stapleton and Smith had missed it, considering the number of people that had been there even before they got there.

"I think it's safe to say that we are looking for a rich killer. You don't see these boots anywhere these days." Dr. Peralta was truly intrigued by the killer's personality.

"The doctor is right. They are Swiss." Tony Adolf had stayed behind. Chief Horning allowed him. "My father gave me a pair of those before he died, but my dog chewed off one of the pair."

Now, something was forming inside Stapleton's head. Tyron Baker had claimed that the truck he saw was old modeled, the knife and now the boots. At this point, the killer seemed to him like air, he was gone even as you felt him.

Chapter 10

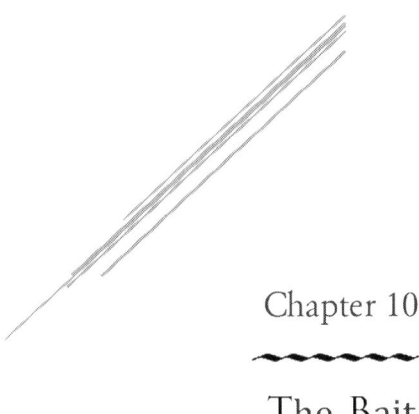

The Bait

Paul Griffith was the first visitor they had in the KPD the next day. The media was in a frenzy about the death of Elise Mckennie. It was now the fourth death of the same kind. The mayor could not contain himself anymore, especially now that his niece was the only one left to be killed. Even the state government was taking interest in the case now. Chief Horning spoke with some FBI agents earlier that day over the phone. They were coming in by next week.

Elise Mckennie's death had made the national news. The mayor wanted Kirtland to make the national news, but certainly not for reasons such as this.

"Chief Horning, please where exactly are we on this

case?" Paul asked, with concern on his face.

"I assure you that our best hands are working tirelessly to catch this killer. It's just a matter of time before we have a breakthrough."

"We don't have time. Very soon the whole world will be breathing down on our necks and by then we won't be able to do our jobs comfortably. Are you sure it's just that one person that is killing these young women?"

"We're certain, sir. My people have established a strong profile. It's only a matter of time."

"If you have to tear down the town to find this person, please do. And I mean that. You have everything at your disposal. If there's anything you need, do not waste any second, call my office."

"Thank you, sir."

Paul Griffith left the KPD building.

Stapleton and Smith did not need to be told that the mayor was expecting something as quickly as possible. Stapleton thought all night about the case. What could they do with the clues they have? The answer had been nothing. It was unchanged as he discussed with his partner until a connection occurred to him. He had been distracted by the case so much, he did not pay attention to some red signs before him.

He had thought so highly of this killer, revered him even that he expected to climb through mountains to catch him. It's time he needed to examine everything before him.

"What do you know about Harold Franczyk?" he asked his partner in the middle of their discussion about the fact that nothing was known to be missing during Mary Logan and Elise Mckennie's murders.

"Nothing much about him. But the Franczyk family used to be really famous in Kirtland. They were stinking rich but Harold is now the only Franczyk that remained in Kirtland."

"I met him at the mayor's birthday party. We talked for a brief moment while you were gone. I saw him again that morning when I returned to Mary Logan's crime scene. He was around the area. He claimed to be exercising past the area. Now that I think about it, he just about fits the profile." Stapleton was getting onto something, and Smith was listening closely to catch it. He did immediately. The process was a revelation not only for Smith, but also for Stapleton.

Everything he had been thinking about, he had done

so in pieces but talking to Smith now, he was piecing them together.

He continued, "I thought he was an interesting young man from our meeting at the party. I didn't know why I was drawn to him but now I think I know. I invited him to lunch for Friday as friends and he declined. He claimed he had an engagement. That was the exact word he used."

Smith kept following his partner. He noted the last part and was quick to understand what Stapleton implied, "Elise Mckennie was killed yesterday, it was a Friday."

"Correct. Now if he got his money through his parents, it wouldn't be a surprise if he was also left with those antiques, but before we go further, let's confirm if he was at Kirtland High around the same time as the girls."

"I bet he was."

Stapleton also shared his partner's belief. He was certain he was there around that time. He still could not believe he knew the killer all this while. But he was ready for that now. He was going to catch him first, then regret later.

Smith brought out the documents from Kirtland High. He was practically looking for the name in their sets, not checking if it was there. When he found it, he showed it to his partner. He was not only at Kirtland High School during the same time as the girls, he was in the same home room as them. Stapleton smiled. There goes their first real win over this case.

"Do we still have the photo albums from the school?" Stapleton asked.

"Yes, it's there." Smith rushed over to the table where it was and brought it back for them to go through.

Harold was not in any of the photos, at least they were not able to put his face on anyone. Then Smith found a photo album of their class. The individuals in the photos were numbered and their names were written below, after their corresponding numbers.

They were speechless to see how Harold Franczyk looked when he was in high school.

"Maybe they made an error." Smith turned to Stapleton.

"No error here, Smith, it explains a lot of things. If he was often bullied in high school, it might have made him feel like an outcast, like they hated him and you see,"

Stapleton got into his animated mode, "Girls like these ones were the prettiest and the most popular in the school. He might have developed a form a hatred towards them. That's the personal touch we've been looking for."

"So, how do we catch this man?"

"Now that's the right question." Stapleton had been thinking about a plan since the beginning of their conversation about Harold Franczyk. Time was not on their side. He did not want some FBI agent to come down here and claim to solve the crime after they had finally reached a breakthrough, so by Monday, he wanted to have Harold Franczyk in custody.

"We can't establish a motive to arrest him, at least we don't have the time."

"But we could search his home for the knife, if it matches the fragment that we found."

"That's too risky. What if he had discarded it? He's gonna know we are onto him and we won't be able to arrest him."

"What of the boots and the truck?"

"Same thing applies, besides, those are circumstantial. They could be anybody's. Tony Adolf said he had one, who knows the number of people that have something similar, regardless of how rare they say it is." Stapleton sat down. "The thing is, it is better we catch him directly with the crime at this stage, rather than standing through the test of circumstantial evidence."

Smith reasoned with his partner. He was right, it could drag on and on. What they needed was to close this case once and celebrate over it, if they could. After all the killings, he doubted they could. He remembered his days as a rookie detective. He celebrated every successful case with Maureen. It was one of the happiest moments of his life. He shook it off. He concentrated back to work.

"So, what do you suggest we do?" he asked Stapleton. He seemed to have one or two things under his sleeves.

"It involves a lot of factors but if we are able to put them together, I believe we have our man."

"What is it like?"

"I say we bait him."

"How?"

"As it stands, he'd be looking to kill Sunny too. He had acted quickly to kill Elise at the campaign ground because that was his only opportunity. He wasted no time in taking it. It shows that he recognizes opportunities and when to take them. We are gonna create an opportunity for him to kill Sunny Griffith and that is how we will catch him."

"But how do we do that? We can't just offer Sunny Griffith to him."

"Of course we can, but not in the way that you think. The last time I spoke to him he said he was ready to have lunch with me another time, but obviously Friday was the issue. He had to kill Elise Mckennie. But before that, we need to return Sunny Griffith to her house, then we station ourselves at the front of her house, we use the KPD wagon to make it obvious. Believe me, for someone who was able to kill those girls in such a way he must have been carefully watching them every minute."

"I still don't understand."

"You will. He sees us watching over Sunny then I call him that he could join me and my partner over lunch by a certain time. Believe me, he'll agree but he won't come or he'd plan to come late. That's his opportunity to kill Sunny. He'd recognize it and take it immediately. I'll make it look like we are looking to slip away from work for an hour. It's risky for him, but killing Elise Mckennie at the campaign ground was risky too. He took the chance anyway. He's gonna want to take this one too."

Stapleton seemed so confident in his plan. It sounded awesome to Smith too but he had his doubts. "What if he doesn't?"

"We have nothing to lose, do we? But you have to trust me on this, he will. I have been waiting for this since we've been on this case, an opportunity to catch him at his own game."

If Smith did not know better, he would have said Stapleton was crazy. "How do we start this plan?" he asked him.

"The earlier the better. Call the mayor's office and invite Sunny Griffith in. Her uncle already requested that two men be placed on her, so she's safe to move. I'll get Chief Horning."

An hour later, Chief Horning and Sunny were already seated with the two detectives in their office. Chief Horning had been briefed earlier about everything the detectives had found out, including their plans. Sunny just came in and she had no knowledge of why she was suddenly invited into the KPD building.

Stapleton did not hesitate to go straight to the point, "Ms. Griffith, do you know Harold Franczyk?"

The question tensed her up, she hoped they did not notice her, or at least, they did not take it into account. "Yes, we went to high school together. Why?"

"We think he's the killer we've been looking for," Stapleton said flatly. He had been wanting to be able to utter a statement of this kind for a long time.

Sunny eyes widened. She shared a different reason for her surprise. Did Harold find out she knew about his mother's death and he had punished her friends for it? That would be crazy! He should have targeted Paul himself and Philip Baker and that Fortune man or whatever his name was. She realized she was still among three policemen, and they expected a reaction from her.

"Why would he do that? Why do you think he's the one?"

"We could stay here and waste time explaining why we think he's the killer or move forward and catch him, then talk later. I'd prefer the latter," Stapleton replied.

"Okay, what do you need me to do?"

"Before that, we have a few questions for you about Harold Franczyk. You guys went to the same high school. How do you see him?"

"I've actually known him since elementary school. Harold was just a normal kid. He hasn't always looked like he looks now. He used to be this… ," she hesitated, searching for the right word.

"Fat." Smith helped her out.

"You could say so," Sunny smiled, not because of what she said, but what she was about to say. "He once asked to be my boyfriend, it was adorable. If I didn't have a boyfriend, I would have gone out with him for a while."

"But you told him no," Stapleton pointed out.

"I told him no. I guess a lot of kids thought he was weird but I thought he was just different. I can't really see why he'd start killing my friends." Sunny knew she was not exactly saying the truth. She could think about a particular reason. His mother's death.

"So, have you had any contact with him since high school?"

"If you mean if we talk, then no. I saw him at Paul's birthday party. I wanted to say hi before the party ended but considering all that went down that night, I didn't."

"Your other friends, what do you know about their relationships with Harold?"

"You mean my dead friends." She felt guilty to be the only living one. "There was no relationship with Harold Franczyk. If he was really the killer then I think we're gonna have to catch him to really know why."

That settled it for Sunny. She needed to see the person that killed her friends and ask him why he chose to kill them rather than tell them what they did. Just a week ago she had been mad about what they had done to Mary. She was with Elise. Now she was here alone, trying to catch their killer. It was crazy all in her head.

She had not even had the time to mourn them properly. She had been running for her own life, trying to not be the next victim.

Stapleton had been talking with Chief Horning and Detective Smith. He was explaining why the information Sunny provided about Harold aligned with why he thought he was the killer. But the Chief expressed his skepticism, "If it turns out that he isn't the killer then it's gonna be the nightmare of us all."

Stapleton reassured him just as he had done with his partner earlier. Since they had no other suspect and time was ticking the Chief agreed to the plan. It came to Sunny's part. They had to tell her what was happening.

Stapleton could see her confused expression. She tried to hide it when she saw that he was looking at her.

"Ms. Griffith, what we are about to ask you to do will not in any way endanger you or anything, in fact, we are going to be there with you all the way." Stapleton tried to be as casual as he could. If he had it his way, he would have told her that the whole plan is rubbish without her and they needed her to come aboard. But that could put her off. He needed to be professional.

Sunny was more confused than she had earlier been. But she was ready to do anything that would ensure they caught the killer, at least for the sake of her four dead friends. Her heart ached at that thought. Anytime she thought about it, it amazed her that she had not gone crazy. Her four dead friends. "What do I need to do gentlemen? Count me in on anything about catching the person that killed my friends." Her voice broke off as she said the last few words. It was building up within her but she needed to be strong. She made up her mind that she would not cry. Not there.

"We are sorry to put you through all these while you haven't even wrapped your head around what is happening. But our plan is time bound and you're a very important part of it. All effort is to catch the killer as soon as possible."

"I understand, Detective. Let's get to it."

"Thank you. We are trying to use you as bait, in a manner of speaking." Stapleton explained his theory of opportunities and taking them to Sunny and he planned to use it to confirm if he was the killer and catch him in the process.

Surprisingly to the men, Sunny agreed easily. She even commented that she thought it was a genius plan. "Since someone will be inside with me, I don't think it's that risky."

"Policemen will be around the vicinity. As soon as we get our killer, the whole place will be buzzing with uniformed men," Chief Horning reassured her. She was his responsibility now as far as he was concerned.

"So, you will be moving back to your apartment today. Detective Smith and I will be in our wagon all through the night. We'll provide you with a radio. You can radio in immediately if you need anything." Stapleton was making sure she understood the process fully. "And lastly before you go, Ms. Griffith, no one else can know about this other than the four of us present here. The smaller the circle the better."

"Of course. I understand completely, Detective." She said her farewell and left.

Chief Horning thanked the detectives and left too, committing everything into their hands. He trusted Stapleton's judgment and character and he left there with more positivity than he had earlier about the case.

It was now left to Stapleton and Smith to get into Harold's head. Specifically, it was left to Stapleton to prove his theory right. They had agreed to wait until seven in the evening of the next day to put a call through to him. They found a number to the Franczyk house on the telephone directory. Stapleton wrote it down.

"Let's get prepared for tonight's vigil," Smith said to his partner to ease him up. He could feel his uptightness. He was beginning to think that if the plan failed, it would all be on him.

Harold heard the telephone ring. It was the one downstairs. Anytime it rang, it was always either some of her mother's business associates or someone who did not know she was dead yet. Or his uncle from New York, whom he had no business with. He had never seen the man before but he had claimed to have carried him while he was a baby. Then why was he not around for his sister's funeral? He had no answer to that. Family nonsense.

Harold picked up the phone.

"Hello, Harold? Harold Franczyk?"

"Yes. Who's asking?"

"It's me, Stapleton, Wayne Stapleton. Remember me? Party lover?"

Of course, he knew who he was. Detective Stapleton.

"Oh, hi! I'm sorry about the other day. I had something important to do. How did you get this number?"

"No problem. I looked it up in the telephone directory. Did I tell you I'm a cop?"

"Oh, I see. No, you didn't."

"I'm trying to get away from work with my partner for lunch tomorrow. Thought I'd use that opportunity to run you through a second invite."

"Tomorrow sounds nice. I'm free. What time?"

"Say, 2pm? Fine by you?"

"Cool, I'll be there."

"Yes. Same address on the note I gave you. Bye, Harold."

"Yeah, bye."

Smith wished he could hear the voices on the other side of the telephone. As soon as Stapleton dropped the phone, he jumped off his feet. "He took the bait?"

"Yes, he did!"

"Thank goodness. Now let's hope he follows through as we'd expect him to."

"He's gonna show up at Sunny's apartment and not the restaurant. He was too eager to accept my invitation. He said he'll be there even before I told him I put an address on the note I gave him the other day. A note I'm sure he discarded the moment I gave him."

It appeared that he really was going to be trapped by this plan. "Should we inform the chief?"

"Yes, but remember we still have to keep up appearances at Sunny's house tonight."

"Yeah and by tomorrow we prepare for lunch."

***

At exactly 1:55pm, Harold appeared on Alpine Drive. He did not come with the truck. He came with a bicycle. He saw that the detectives' vehicle was really not in the area. Since Sunny had decided not to go to work in order to mourn her friends, they thought they should abandon detective work and keep watch over her. Harold smiled at the thought. Now they wanted to fill their bellies and run away from her, just like everyone else in her life. If only Sunny could understand that and embrace him. He would never desert her. That bastard Jackson Hayes betrayed her, her friends betrayed her, her uncle used her. Her life was just as lonely as his. The glamour around her had blinded her from seeing that. If only she could see how similar they were. That they were not that different from each other and that they were meant for each other. But it was too late now, she chose her path. She was going to face the music.

The area was residential but virtually everyone that lived around worked nine to five jobs. He had studied the area just like he had studied others. There was a field far behind Sunny's house. It had a lot of trees. He hid there anytime he came there to observe the area.

He was not going to move Sunny's body. He had to take this opportunity as it is. He still planned on joining the detectives. So, he needed to move quickly. He advanced towards the house. It was a lone apartment, no neighbors. There was no rear door. The second door led to the garage area, so he had to make use of the front door.

He brought out his pocket knife of different blades and tried his trick but the door did not open. After he had tried a couple of times more, he kicked the door open.

Sunny ran out to him. Harold saw that she looked dressed, the skirt was dark blue, his favorite color. Harold thought she looked stunning. He had waited for this day for so long and now he felt confused standing in the same room with her.

"Harold Franczyk, why have you killed my four friends? I just need to know why!" Sunny's voice was cracking. She was going to cry.

Harold could not utter a word. He wanted to tell her how evil her friends were and how they had corrupted her with this evilness.

"Guess, you're not gonna say anything, uh?" She was about to charge at him when Stapleton grabbed her.

A wave of shock hit Harold and he fell on the floor. He could not believe he had been fooled easily by the detective. He had thought he was on top of them all this while.

The expression on his face was what Stapleton wanted to see, the expression of someone that was caught at his game. Sunny's living room was instantly filled with uniformed men, coming from every angle. Sirens were blaring outside loudly.

Chief Horning and Smith smiled at each other. They looked at Stapleton, who was cuffing Harold and they had a new form of respect for the man. His resilience had got them this far. If not for him, Harold would still be a free man, after he probably would have added Sunny to his list.

Sunny kept crying. She could not believe what was happening. She screamed out suddenly, "Ask him why he did it, please! Somebody ask him! Weirdo! This was why everyone called you weirdo. Monster!"

Stapleton went back to Sunny and pleaded with her. "Everything you want to know will be revealed. He's now in custody. We'll carry out a thorough investigation. Please be patient. You've been so brave since all this beginning and you've lost four friends in the space of a few weeks, that's traumatic for anyone. Please, Ms. Griffith." Stapleton led her away from the crowd.

About The Authors

To date, Donald and Cathy have written six children's books, illustrated in color and available in eBook, Paperback and Audio. This novel, The Kirtland Killer, is their second full-length crime mystery book.

Donald and Cathy live in Peoria, Arizona. Cathy is a homemaker and Donald is a retired Manufacturing Manager and former Elementary Governing Board Member in Phoenix, Arizona.

For additional information including ordering and social media links:

Website: www.dcrushbooks.com

Author Page: http://www.amazon.com/-/e/B00B0T04SI

Facebook: www.facebook.com/dcrushbooks
Pinterest: www.pinterest.com/dcrushbooks/
Twitter: www.twitter.com/dcrushbooks
Linkedin: www.linkedin.com/in/dcrushbooks
YouTube: www.youtube.com/c/DCRush
Instagram: www.instagram.com/dcrushbooks/

Made in the USA
Monee, IL
15 June 2022